THE
PATH
THROUGH
THE TREES

Peggy Dymond Leavey

Napoleon

Toronto, Ontario, Canada

Text © 2005 Peggy Dymond Leavey

All rights reserved. No part of this publication may be reproduced, stored in a retrieval system or transmitted, in any form or by any means, electronic, mechanical, photocopying, recording or otherwise, without the prior consent of the publisher.

Cover art by Patty Gallinger

Published by Napoleon Publishing
Toronto, Ontario, Canada

Le Conseil des Arts | The Canada Cou
du Canada | for the Arts

Napoleon Publishing acknowledges the support of the Canada Council for our publishing program.

Printed in Canada

09 08 07 06 05 5 4 3 2 1

Library and Archives Canada Cataloguing in Publication

Leavey, Peggy Dymond
    The path through the trees / Peggy Dymond Leavey.

ISBN 1-894917-21-9

    I. Title.

PS8573.E2358P38 2005   jC813'.54   C2004-
907038-XPZ7

For Zoë

The most beautiful things in the world we cannot see, or even touch. They are felt within our heart.
-Helen Keller

One

*J*ody didn't know what had called him to return. A feeling deep inside him, something like longing, had drawn him back to the little shed in the woods.

He had to use the side of his shoe to scrape all the mud and leaves from the doorway, before finally pushing open the door. In the pale light of mid-December, he saw that everything was as he'd left it—the coal oil lantern that hung from a nail over the workbench, the trusty little woodstove, its pipe thrust up through the roof. The box with the rope handles still held his tools. Even the narrow cot under the window looked undisturbed. It was only when he shook out the blanket covering the cot that he discovered it had been home to a family of mice.

Never mind, he thought. He'd take the pipes down and bang the soot out of them. Then he'd get a fire going in the little stove. It had always been sufficient to heat this small space. He'd have it cozy in no time. Even the field mice were welcome to stay, provided they found a corner of their own and left the cot for him.

Jody had been down to the big house only once since his return, and he hadn't seen the lady there. He'd go down

1

again later and have another look around. He wondered if she might be sick. Could that be the reason he'd been summoned to return?

He picked up the straw broom that stood in the corner and busied himself sweeping the floor. Through the sound of the rain pattering on the carpet of leaves outside came the whistle of the train as it approached the level crossing. Jody lifted his head and listened.

*   *   *

Norah Bingham stood alone on the station platform. The throbbing of the train, now disappearing into the distance, filled her head. She had the sensation that her body still rocked from side to side with its rhythm.

A single yellow taxi waited in the rain. Where, she wondered, was Great-aunt Caroline?

The driver got out of the cab and watched as she approached—a thin girl, wearing jeans and a hip-length navy jacket. She was dragging a nylon suitcase on wobbly wheels and skirting the puddles.

"A girl, the lady told me," the man acknowledged, giving a hitch to his jeans. "And seeing's you're the only one who got off, you must be her." He reached out for the suitcase.

Norah hesitated, peeling a damp strand of wind-blown hair from across her mouth. "I understood Miss Caroline Stoppard was to meet me."

"Well, you understood wrong," the man grunted. He seized the suitcase and slung it onto the back seat of the cab. "Miz Stoppard paid me to fetch you, and that's what I'm doing. So get in, please. No sense standing out here getting wet."

Seeing as her luggage was going wherever the yellow taxi was, Norah had no choice but to climb into the cab beside the suitcase. The driver closed her door and slid in again under the wheel. "Don't know how you figured Miz Stoppard could come and fetch you," he muttered, adjusting the mirror so that Norah could see his eyes. "She hasn't had that car of hers out of the garage in years."

The cab jolted and splashed its way through the potholes in the parking lot and out onto the street. After passing the untidy sprawl of a lumberyard, it made a right turn onto a side street and a left onto the highway.

A fried chicken place at the corner was filling the air with the most mouth-watering aroma, reminding Norah that all she'd eaten that day was the hot dog her mother had bought her at Union Station before she'd boarded the one o'clock train.

And that reminded her of their conversation just before she left. "Haven't you always dreamed of a Christmas like you see in the movies, Norah honey?" Her mother's blue eyes were moist. "You know, the little houses and streets all trimmed with snow? That's the way it could be in Pinegrove."

"Mom, that movie snow is mostly fake! I heard they made it out of soap. And the streets are likely in California someplace. Didn't you wonder how that ditzy family could all stand around outside in their pajamas, watching the dad string the lights? It was totally fake!"

Now, from the back of the taxi, Norah craned to see what there was of the little town of Pinegrove. "I'm not sure exactly where my aunt lives," she admitted. "I thought she'd be the one picking me up."

"Oh, the lady doesn't live in the village. Her place is a coupla miles out." The driver was watching her. "Miz Stoppard a relative of yours?"

"My father's aunt," Norah replied, peering out through the rain. With the exception of the train station and the lumberyard, the town was just one street deep. Small houses straggled along the highway as far as the "Come Back Soon" sign. There, they petered out altogether, and bare fields and trees took over.

"You here all by yourself?" The cabbie was inquisitive.

"My mom's coming in a couple of days," Norah replied. "And my cousins will be here for Christmas." She saw the eyebrows in the mirror rise.

"That so? Miz Stoppard doesn't get much company, as a rule. She's a bit of a recluse, you might say." He pronounced it as if it were two words.

"My mom thought it would be nice for all of us to be together for Christmas this year." Norah didn't bother telling the man that up until a month ago, neither she nor her mother knew that Great-aunt Caroline was even still alive.

"We invited her to come and spend the holidays with us. But when she said she couldn't, Mom decided we would bring the festivities to her."

"That so. And what did she say to that?"

Norah traced a drop of condensation as it slid down

the window beside her. "She said she had a big house and had never been known to turn anyone away." Which was not exactly what you could call an invitation. When Norah had pointed that out to her mother, Ginny had only laughed. "It'll be perfect, Norah. You'll see. Wonderful fun." Everything always was, for Ginny. As far as Norah was concerned, nothing was turning out the way it was supposed to.

Ever since Ginny had learned that she and Norah would be leaving Victoria and moving east to Toronto, she had been going on about living closer to her brother Richard and his wife and two children. "For the first time in years, Norah, our family can spend the holidays together," Ginny had crowed.

When Ginny discovered that her late husband's aunt was still living in Ontario, she came up with the idea of inviting her too. It didn't matter that the old lady was no relation to Uncle Richard, Auntie Gwen or the cousins.

Then, at the last minute, still surrounded by packing crates in their new apartment, Ginny had been called back out west. Some urgent problem the person who was taking over was having, and only Ginny could fix it. Now what? Christmas was only a week away.

"It's really no problem, sweetie," Ginny promised. "I'll just call Aunt Caroline and see if you can go on up there ahead of me. And I'll join you the minute I get back."

"I'll go with you, Mom," Norah decided. "I know I could stay at Ashley's."

"No, it'll be much quicker if I just do what has to be done and fly right back."

"Let me stay here then," Norah pleaded. "I could have all the unpacking done by the time you get back."

Ginny shook her head. "I don't know a soul in this city I could ask to stay with you, darling. No, this way is best. I'll get you a ticket for the train. And here's an idea! Why don't we call Richard and see if the kids can go on ahead too? You three could be all together for a while."

"I bet Andrew and Becca are looking forward to this holiday about as much as I am," grumbled Norah.

When she'd called her brother in Guelph, Ginny had learned that school for the cousins was not yet out for the Christmas break. The only reason Norah was already on holiday was that she would be starting Grade Eight in a new school after the New Year.

"I guess you'll just have to go on ahead by yourself," Ginny announced, setting the phone back down on the floor beside the couch where she and Norah were unwrapping dishes. She picked up another package, smiling brightly. "But that's okay. I'm sure your Great-aunt Caroline will spoil you rotten."

By this time, the taxi had turned off the highway between two stone pillars and into a lane overhung with dripping trees. A large house of grey stone loomed ahead in the cold rain. The cab pulled up at the front of the house and stopped.

This place was not what Norah had imagined when her mother had promised Christmas in the country. She had pictured a rambling house of white clapboard, a wide, welcoming verandah, coloured lights strung from gingerbread trim, a wreath in every lighted window. And snow, of course.

"Well, this is it," the cabbie announced, opening the back door of the car.

Norah emerged from the taxi an inch at a time, looking up at the gloomy house, its chimneys wrapped in fog.

There was no verandah, no front porch of any kind, and no lights beckoned from the unfriendly windows. In fact, the place looked deserted. In the trees to the left, Norah spotted a detached garage with old-fashioned, wooden doors.

After depositing the suitcase on the stone step, the driver got back into the cab and splashed away again down the lane, without even waiting to see if anyone answered the door.

Norah had just about decided that no one was home and was half-hoping that they weren't, when the big front door swung suddenly inward.

"Come inside," an icy voice commanded. "Don't just stand there. You're letting in the rain."

Two

A t first, Norah thought the woman who answered the door of the dreary, stone house was very tall. Later, she realized that was due to the straightness of her posture. She wore a long, black skirt, polished shoes of the same colour and a grey blouse with a high throat, buttoned to the top. Her white hair was pulled back in a severe style behind her head. A pair of rimless spectacles perched halfway down a long, narrow nose.

Norah wiped her hand on her jeans and extended it towards the woman. "I'm Norah," she announced with a smile. The door closed behind her.

"Of course you are." The woman stepped back and took a long look at Norah's wet shoes. "You may hang your things there," she said, indicating a hallstand, the kind with a seat that opened and a place for umbrellas.

Norah dropped her hand. "Is my Aunt Caroline home?" she asked.

"I am Caroline Stoppard," declared the woman, unsmiling.

"Oh, I'm sorry," Norah exclaimed. "It's just, you know, with a house as big as this, I thought you might be…"

"The maid?" Cold, blue eyes peered at Norah over the spectacles. "Perfectly understandable. How could you be expected to know me, when we have never met?"

Feeling it was better to say nothing at all, Norah hung her jacket over one of the hooks on the hallstand and stepped out of her shoes.

Once that was properly done, Caroline Stoppard walked briskly across the hall to the foot of the stairs. "Come along now," she said. "There are no servants in this house. I will show you to your room."

Lugging the suitcase, Norah followed the erect figure up the stairs, sneaking a look at her surroundings as she climbed. The stairs were painted black, uncarpeted, and they swept in a wide arc to a landing, halfway to the second floor. A circular window of red and blue glass spilled a watery stain onto the hardwood at their feet. There were no paintings, no family portraits on the grey walls as Norah might have expected. The house appeared as cold and unadorned as its owner.

"Your mother is coming when, exactly?" Aunt Caroline asked, waiting for Norah to catch up.

"The day after tomorrow," Norah puffed. "She was called away on business."

"Well, I suppose that can't be helped," was the comment.

At the top of the stairs, they turned into a dark hallway. Aunt Caroline opened a door to a room at the front of the house and stepped aside to allow Norah to enter first. It was cold as a tomb inside.

"This will be your room," the woman announced.

"I've put some towels in here for you to use. The bathroom is down the hall, on the left. You may put your clothes in the bureau over there."

Wheeling the suitcase to a spot inside the door, Norah scanned the room. There was one, curtainless window in the opposite wall. A massive oak dresser that Aunt Caroline had called a bureau occupied most of the wall on the left. The floor of the room was bare except for a rectangle of beige carpet next to the bed. That bit of carpet, the mirror over the dresser and a small lamp on top of the bookcase were the room's only decorative touches.

Hands clasped primly at her waist, Aunt Caroline watched as Norah's eyes swept the room. "I am not used to children," the woman said. "So we'll just try to get along the best we can, shall we?"

"I'm not exactly a child," Norah pointed out. She was trying to be polite, although her great-aunt's words had stung. "I was thirteen on my last birthday."

A smile flickered briefly over the colourless lips. "Supper is at six." And with that she was gone, leaving Norah with only the sound of her sensible shoes descending the stairs.

Norah crossed the room to the window. She looked out at the muddy lane she had just travelled and an overgrown lawn, matted with soggy, brown leaves. She had not expected to be relegated to her room so soon. Shouldn't there be a few little welcoming gestures first? Make yourself at home; have some milk and cookies? This was the person her mother thought would spoil her?

The big bed in the middle of the room was so high

that Norah had to hop up to sit on it. From there she could reach the lamp on the bookcase. Norah switched it on. The yellow light it shed seemed to soften some of the sharp angles of the room.

She checked out the shelves of the bookcase and found them crammed with old books, their cloth spines faded to one monotonous shade of rust. Nothing interesting there.

Sliding off the bed, Norah closed the door to the hall and stood leaning against it, angry at her mother and even more angry at herself for going along with Ginny's plan. She should have fought harder against it. She could have been on her way to Ashley's right now.

Norah carried the suitcase to the wide sill of the window and unzipped it. She had already made up her mind that she would not unpack. Not yet, not if there was any chance of an early escape.

Looking at her familiar old clothes, the books she had tucked in along the edge of the suitcase, and remembering her mother carefully folding everything for her, filled her with a sudden ache of loneliness. How was she ever going to put in two whole days by herself in this awful place?

The drawers of the dresser, which Norah pulled open out of curiosity, were all lined with clean, white paper. She was relieved to discover in the bottom drawer a folded, woollen blanket. Maybe she could sleep the rest of this horrible afternoon away.

Three

Norah awoke to find the temperature of the room she had been assigned in Great-aunt Caroline's house more frigid than ever. She slid off the bed, pulling the scratchy blanket around her. She dug her slippers out of a side pocket on the suitcase and shoved her feet into them.

Opening the door to the hall, Norah was surprised to discover it was much warmer than the bedroom. Along with the heat, the unexpected aroma of cooking food wafted up the stairs. There was something comforting about the smell of food cooking, and it cheered her a little. Or perhaps it was the nap that made her feel more optimistic. By now, Aunt Caroline might be used to the idea of having a teenaged houseguest. They just needed to give each other a second chance.

Every door along the hall, as well as the one to the right of the stairs, was closed. No wonder the hallway was so dark. A window at the far end looked down on a narrow sideyard, a wooden fence lined with the stalks of dead hollyhocks and beyond, a forest of naked trees. Creepy, Norah decided.

She exchanged the blanket for a towel from her room

and found the bathroom behind one of the closed doors. Norah let the water run into the sink until it was finally warm. Holding her hands under it, she splashed a little over her face.

The fine braids that held the sides of her straight, brown hair back behind her ears had come undone, and she rebraided them in front of the mirror, clipping the ends together at the back of her head. She took a moment to stare in the glass at her pale face with its sharp features, the nose she thought too long, the brown eyes a little too close together.

"Well, here you are, Norah Bingham," she said to her reflection. "Whether you like it or not."

*　　*　　*

"I can't believe you're doing this, Mom," she had said earlier that afternoon, as she and Ginny stood in the line-up at gate seven in Union Station, waiting for the train to points east. "You don't even know this woman, and now you're sending your only child off to stay with her, all by herself!"

"Come on, Norah." Ginny gave her a good-natured nudge. "This is your father's aunt. I know enough about her that I'm confident you'll be well looked after. I'm sure she's a lovely person."

"You think everybody's a lovely person," Norah muttered. "Even that guy in the next apartment, who looks to me like a hit man for the Mafia."

Ginny smiled nervously at the woman sitting on her

suitcase ahead of them in the line, listening to every word. "Oh, Norah, what an imagination! Try to make the best of this little setback, dear. We're still going to have a holiday in the country."

*   *   *

Leaving the door to the bathroom open, Norah descended the stairs to the ground floor. She peeked into the room to the right of the front entrance. It contained several pieces of leather furniture, looking creased and comfortable. There was even a television set in one corner. "Well, this is better," she said, under her breath.

Across the hall was a formal living room, its windows covered with heavy draperies. The needlepoint seatcovers on several side chairs provided the only relief to the drab colour scheme.

An arch connected the living room to the dining room. Light leaked from under a door to the right. Norah knew by the smells coming from that room that it must be the kitchen. Her stomach rolled with hunger.

The dining room windows looked out over a backyard bordered by a hedge of overgrown cedar trees. Norah crossed the room to look outside.

In the far corner of the yard, and leaning slightly to one side, was a dilapidated gazebo. Halfway along the hedge, an opening had been left to the forest behind it.

Night was falling beyond the cedars, but the backyard itself was well lit. To Norah's surprise, she saw that the yard was practically filled with birdfeeders. They hung from the branches of every tree, from the clothesline, the gazebo and from numerous hooks driven here and there into the ground. There were dozens of them, in every imaginable shape and size.

Moving closer to the window for a better look, Norah was startled to see that there was someone out there.

A figure was standing in the rain at the opening in the cedar hedge. A boy, she thought, by the size of him, and he was watching her.

Four

Norah took a quick step away from the window where she'd been surveying the yard and nearly collided with Aunt Caroline, who chose that exact moment to come though the swinging door from the kitchen.

"My goodness!" exclaimed the woman, irritably. "Don't jump out at me like that!"

"Sorry," said Norah. "I was just looking at your backyard. For a minute, I thought I saw someone out there." After a second glance, she wasn't so sure.

"I doubt it," Aunt Caroline sniffed. "No one comes out this far, especially in the rain."

Great-aunt Caroline wiped her hands on the striped apron she wore and reached behind the drapes to switch off the outside lights. Immediately, the scene beyond the window jumped back, leaving only their reflections in the glass and that of the room around them.

Could Norah have imagined the boy she saw standing there? She had only seen him for a moment. But why would her eyes play tricks on her?

"I've never seen so many birdfeeders all in one place, Aunt Caroline," she said, remembering that she was going to start over with her great-aunt and putting on a smile. "It's amazing!"

"Amazing, is it? Well, it's a fair bit of work too," the woman admitted. "I get juncos, blue jays, cardinals." She counted them off on long, thin fingers. "Grosbeaks, nuthatches, more varieties every year. And squirrels too, of course. I used to put up baffles to keep the squirrels off the feeders, but now I just make sure there's enough food to satisfy all the little creatures. They know they can count on being fed here."

"In the morning, I'll go out and have a look around myself," said Norah. She wondered if the next day there'd be any way of telling whether there had been someone in the yard.

"There's not much to look at," Aunt Caroline told her in a sour tone. "The only thing I grew this year were sunflowers. The birds appreciate them, anyway. The rest of the plants come up in spite of my neglect. Fortunately, I have no neighbours to complain about all the weeds."

"It must be a lot of work for one person," Norah agreed. "Is there anything I could do now to help you with supper? Maybe I could set the table. Do you eat in here, or in the kitchen?"

"I take my meals here in the dining room." Aunt Caroline drew herself up to her full height again. "You'll find mats for the table in the drawer of the buffet, cutlery in the top drawer on the right."

Since there was no invitation to join her aunt in the kitchen, where she knew it would be warmer, Norah hurried upstairs and dragged a sweatshirt out of her suitcase before returning to set the table.

Ten minutes later, emerging from the kitchen with a bowl of steaming stew, Aunt Caroline noticed the sweatshirt. "You're cold," she accused, frowning.

"A little," Norah admitted. "I had a nap, and I always feel chilled when I wake up. Don't you?"

"I do not take naps during the daytime, unless I am ill." The woman spooned some stew onto Norah's plate and looked at her over the top of her eyeglasses, adding, "You're not ill, I hope."

"No, I'm fine." Norah set her fork back onto the table. "But I was wondering, Aunt Caroline, there doesn't seem to be any heat in that bedroom."

"If you leave your door open, you'll be warm enough," the woman said. "I trust the room suits you, otherwise?"

"Oh, yes. It's fine."

The woman nodded. "It was good enough for me when I was a girl."

"Really? It was your room? Then, you've always lived here?"

"I have. This house was built for my father." Great-aunt Caroline set her mouth into a straight line again and peered critically at the food that remained on Norah's plate.

Norah returned her attention to the meal. The stew, if not her hostess, was warm and delicious. There was homemade bread to go with it and a fragrant spice cake for dessert.

"You're a very good cook, Aunt Caroline," Norah said, sitting back against her chair and putting her hands on her full stomach. "I'll help you with the dishes whenever you're ready to do them."

"No, thank you." Her great-aunt rose from the table. "I suggest you go find a book to read." She hesitated. "You do read, don't you?"

Norah gave a little laugh. "Of course."

"Well, it's just that I heard with all your TVs and computers, children don't read these days. More's the pity."

"We still read," Norah protested. "I brought two books with me, in fact. I love to curl up with a book. But I want to help you, if you'll let me."

"Well, that's considerate of you, I suppose, but I am used to managing on my own," Aunt Caroline retorted. And just before she disappeared through the swinging door, "You may bring your book into the kitchen, if you wish."

Norah didn't wait to be asked a second time. She flew from the room and was back downstairs with one of her paperbacks in two minutes, plopping into a rocking chair in the kitchen beside the stove. The wood in its belly crackled companionably.

Aunt Caroline washed dishes in silence for a few minutes. "I think you'd better tell me about these cousins of yours that are coming," she suggested grudgingly. She didn't turn from the sink. "Are they noisy children?"

Norah looked up in surprise. "No more than other kids," she said, talking to her great-aunt's back. "I guess you could say Becca gets a bit hyper at times, but she's only ten. Andrew's sort of serious."

The sound of gentle splashing continued from the sink.

"Andrew is the same age as me," Norah continued. "I think his birthday is in January. You know, Mom and I hadn't seen them in such a long time, and then Uncle

Richard brought them out west last summer. It was their first time seeing the Rockies and the coast. After that, we started emailing each other all the time."

Putting a finger in the book to mark her place, Norah went on, "It's always been just Mom and me. But lately, Mom's had this thing about reconnecting with any relatives we have. That's why she wrote to you." She saw Aunt Caroline reach for a towel from behind the stove. "You wouldn't happen to remember my dad, would you?" Norah asked, hopefully.

The woman took a plate from the dish rack and began to dry it vigorously. "He was my sister's child. They lived down east."

"I know. I can't remember him either," Norah admitted with a sigh. "Sometimes I think I can, and then I see a picture of him with me when I was little, and I know it's the picture I remember. I was only two when he died. I wish you had gotten to know him." She didn't add what she was thinking—that at least it would give them something to talk about.

"Well, we all have our own lives to live," declared Aunt Caroline. She finished wiping up around the sink, untied the apron and hung it behind the door. "Come along now. We're finished in here," she announced. She had her hand on the light switch already.

Without another word, they left the kitchen. As she passed the buffet in the dining room, Aunt Caroline picked up a wicker sewing basket and proceeded with it through the living room and across the hall to the den. Norah followed on her heels. She stopped beside the television. "May I turn it on?" she asked.

"You could if it worked," replied Aunt Caroline, placing a cushion against the back of one of the leather chairs and lowering herself into it.

"Oh. Well, maybe when they get here, one of the grownups can take it somewhere and get it fixed for you."

"Whatever for?" Aunt Caroline puzzled, scowling. "I never had television before, and I don't need it now. I just wish someone would take the thing away."

"I thought it might be company for you," Norah suggested.

"How on earth can something as one-sided as television be company?" Aunt Caroline demanded. She opened the basket and drew out a square of half-finished needlework. "Anyway, someone I rented a room to at one time brought it with him. Said he was going to share it with me and had the nerve to set it up in here. It never did work."

She glared at Norah, who had not moved from the side of the offending television set. "Don't you have any handwork you could be doing?"

"Handwork?"

"Something to keep your hands busy in the evenings. I always have something I can pick up, rather than sitting idle."

"Maybe I'll just go up to bed," Norah suggested. Anything was better than sitting here under Aunt Caroline's critical eye. She saw the disapproving look her great-aunt gave the clock, ticking out the hollow seconds on the mantle. "I know it's only seven-thirty, but I'm still kind of tired from the trip."

"Of course you are," Aunt Caroline conceded, in a gentler tone. She was probably relieved, Norah thought, that the two of them wouldn't have to make conversation all evening.

Upstairs, having changed into her pajamas, Norah opened the door of the bedroom and climbed into bed with her book. But instead of reading, she let her mind go back over the afternoon, looking for chinks in the armour Aunt Caroline wore. It was only when she was telling Norah about her birds that Norah had glimpsed a warmer side to her great-aunt.

* * *

There was no moon to light the path as Jody made his way back to the shed in the woods. In spite of all the years that had passed since the last time he'd been here, the route from the big house was still familiar to him.

Once in out of the rain, the embers of the fire in his little stove provided enough light for him to find the tin of matches. Striking one, he held it to the wick of the lantern, adjusting the flame before he hung it back on the nail over the bench.

The lady had looked well enough, he thought. Older, but that was to be expected after all this time. But what about this girl he'd seen with her? Could she be the reason he'd felt drawn to come back here? Maybe the girl was the one who would provide him with another chance to connect with the family. But who was she?

Five

The first thing Norah heard the next morning was the sound of freezing rain peppering the eaves. Tiny icicles hung from the trees and coated the wires into the house. The only good thing about the dismal scene from the bedroom window, in Norah's opinion, was that the temperature must be falling, and that might mean there would be snow for Christmas.

It was past eight o'clock by the time Norah had dressed and hurried downstairs. Aunt Caroline had already disappeared somewhere into the silence of the house. There was one place set for breakfast at the table in the dining room. A fortress of little boxes of dry cereal ringed the place mat, and there was a glass of pale juice that turned out not to be orange, but grapefruit. It puckered her mouth. Norah took the glass with her to the window and looked out.

She was surprised to discover her great-aunt in the backyard, her clothing covered by an enormous black raincoat. Moving carefully over the frozen ground, Caroline Stoppard was making the rounds of the ice-coated birdfeeders. Norah watched as she threaded her way between the feeding stations, filling each one with a scoop cut from a plastic bleach bottle that she dipped into a garbage can of seed on the back step.

And there, watching her, was the boy. Norah was positive it was the same person she'd seen last evening. This time, he was standing inside the hedge, holding the collar of his short jacket closed with one hand, his shoulders hunched against the bitter rain. Aunt Caroline seemed unaware of him.

Norah felt her pulse quicken in her throat, and she rapped on the window to alert her aunt to his presence. "Over there," she mouthed, pointing, when the woman looked up with a scowl. "That boy, there!"

Aunt Caroline didn't seem to understand. She shook her head and bent to dip the scoop into the pail of birdseed again.

Quickly, Norah set the juice onto the table and strode toward the kitchen. She'd go to the back door where her aunt could hear her. But out of the corner of her eye she saw that the boy had already vanished, slipping away into the trees beyond the hedge.

She met Aunt Caroline coming up the back steps and held the door open for her. "Didn't you see...? Oh, be careful on those stairs!" Norah cried, realizing the coat of ice on the stone.

Aunt Caroline entered the house with a great flapping of the raincoat and stepped out of her rubber boots. "I'm always careful," she snapped. "But my feathered friends will be looking to be fed as soon as this storm's over." She glared at Norah. "Have you had *your* breakfast yet?"

"I was just about to," Norah admitted, as her great-aunt hung the dripping raincoat behind the door. "I didn't think you'd seen that boy out there, so I was trying to warn you."

"Is that what you were hammering on the window about?"

"I wasn't hammering," Norah objected. "I just wanted to get your attention."

"Well, nonetheless, I don't need any broken windows, thank you. And I can assure you I was quite alone out there." Still in her stockinged feet, Aunt Caroline filled a kettle at the sink and set it over an opening in the stove.

"There *was* a boy out there, Aunt Caroline," Norah insisted. "And it wasn't the first time I've seen him either. He was there last night too. It's like he's watching the house."

"Nonsense," her great-aunt scoffed. She sat down in the rocking chair to tie her shoes, then straightened up, slapping her hands against her thighs. "There, now I am ready for my mid-morning cup of tea. When you've finished breakfast, please bring your dishes in to the sink."

Confused and a little angry besides, Norah returned to the dining room. As she had expected, the yard was now deserted. But she *had* seen someone there! What seemed more puzzling even than the appearance of the stranger, was that her aunt refused to believe her. Why would she think she'd make it up? Could it be that the old lady did not want to be reminded about how vulnerable she was, living out here on her own?

When she took her dishes to the kitchen, Norah found Aunt Caroline had set up the ironing board and was pressing the backs of several squares of needlework. She didn't look up.

Aware that the woman preferred to be alone, Norah set her breakfast things into the sink and slipped away to her room upstairs.

The rain was coming from the east and driving against the back of the house. When Norah took her toothbrush into the bathroom, little icy fingers were tapping at the window there, like someone scratching to get in. The thought that a stranger could be watching the house made Norah shiver. Even if he was just a boy. And was it her imagination, or was the boy getting closer to the house each time?

Shortly, she heard Aunt Caroline come upstairs and walk along the hall to open the door of the room next to the bathroom. Norah followed as far as the doorway.

"Oh, my mom would just love to have a spare room like this!" she exclaimed, stepping inside. "We don't know where we're going to put everything in our new apartment."

It was obvious that this was where Aunt Caroline stored everything she wanted out of sight. There was a fold-up bed, a number of stacking chairs, two metal racks of clothing in garment bags, a treadle sewing machine, a dressmaker's dummy, a silver tea service swathed in plastic wrap and row upon row of pictures in frames, standing on the floor, turned face-in. The shelves that lined the walls held boxes of various sizes, all clearly labelled.

"I saw one of those sewing machines in a museum once," Norah remarked. "It's cool how you don't need electricity to run them. Just your own feet."

"Yes, I suppose anything that old is a museum piece," agreed Aunt Caroline, dryly.

Norah's cheeks warmed. "I didn't mean…"

"Why not? It's very old. I haven't used it myself in a very long time." Aunt Caroline opened the flaps on one large cardboard box and set the pieces she had been ironing inside.

"So this is where you keep all your needlework," Norah realized, peering into the box with her. "Did you finish that piece you were working on last night?" She picked up a square of needlepoint, filled with black-eyed Susans and brilliant butterflies. "It's so colourful. Did you ever think about framing some of it, Aunt Caroline? You have enough here that you could decorate the whole house." She met her aunt's scowling gaze. "If you wanted to, I mean."

"Which I don't. As I told you last evening, I do it to keep my hands busy. Nothing more."

Norah was standing next to the row of large, framed canvases on the floor, and she turned the first one around to see the front. It was an oil painting of a vase filled with sunflowers—great, floppy circles of sunshine, dripping petals onto a blue tablecloth. "This is nice," she said and reached to turn the next frame towards her.

"They are all oil paintings," Aunt Caroline informed her. "Please just leave them!"

Norah pulled her hand back as if she had been burned.

"They hung in this house for many years," her great-aunt explained. "But I have no use for such things now."

"Why not?" Norah asked.

"I have my reasons," replied Caroline Stoppard. From the stony look on her aunt's face, Norah knew the subject was closed.

"I thought when you first came in here that you might be looking for your Christmas decorations," Norah tried again. "I could help you find them and take them downstairs."

"Christmas isn't until the twenty-fifth," Caroline Stoppard retorted. "Or it was the last time I looked."

"I know. But that's just five days from now. If you told me which box they're in, maybe I could do the decorating for you. I'm really pretty good at it. Do you get a real tree?"

"You won't find any of that stuff up here, so there's no sense poking about. I haven't bothered celebrating anything in years," the woman declared.

It suddenly occurred to Norah that her father's aunt might recognize another holiday this time of year. "My friend Ashley celebrates Hanukkah," she began. "And in school we learned about…"

"If I bothered with any of it, it would be Christmas," Aunt Caroline snapped, cutting her short. "Come along now. I keep the door to this room shut to conserve heat."

For the rest of the morning Norah lay on her bed, wrapped in the scratchy blanket and nursing hurt feelings. No matter how often she tried to make friends with Caroline Stoppard, her great-aunt did not hide the fact that she resented Norah being there.

Her mind kept returning to the paintings in the spare

room. If her aunt owned such beautiful things, why wouldn't she hang them on the walls, instead of storing them away where they couldn't be seen? What possible reason could she have for taking them down? So many things puzzled her about the woman.

And then there was the boy in the yard. Who was he, and why was he watching the house?

Knowing she would get no answers from Caroline Stoppard, Norah finally picked up one of her books and read it straight through to the end. Her mother would arrive tomorrow. Maybe Ginny would be able to thaw Aunt Caroline's icy exterior.

Six

*U*nless he came up with a better plan to find out who she
was and why she was here, Jody intended to catch the
girl when she was alone sometime and ask her.

He remembered from when he had been here before (not
the first time, when he had come as a companion to Joseph,
but later when Joseph had gone back to university) that
Caroline Stoppard used to go out to work every day. But now
she seemed never to leave the property. How was he going to
meet the girl if the woman was always around?

He wondered if something had happened to Caroline
Stoppard's beautiful car, if that was the reason she stayed
home all the time. He would have to check the garage on his
next visit to the house.

In the years after Joseph had left, Jody used to watch
Caroline Stoppard back the vehicle out of the garage every
morning. She would secure the wooden doors, slide in again
under the steering wheel and drive slowly down the lane,
sunlight glinting on polished metal, the colour of midnight.

He approved of the care she took of the car, having it
washed at the dealership in town every Friday. If he owned
a car like that, he'd take good care of it too. Once in a while

he used to slip into the garage, just to admire the sweeping lines of the vehicle, the gleaming chrome.

Once, out of curiosity, he'd gone into Pinegrove looking for the car, wanting to know where it was she went every day. He was not surprised to discover that she ran the little library in the village.

Then, late every afternoon, Caroline Stoppard would return to the big house. In those days, she always ended her day in her garden, plucking faded blooms or pulling weeds. It puzzled Jody that he never saw her cut any flowers for the house, the way she used to when Joseph was there. While Joseph was visiting, there would be a single, fall chrysanthemum or a purple aster on the young man's tray at every meal.

*   *   *

Great-aunt Caroline and Norah were eating lunch, in silence as usual, when for the first time since Norah's arrival, the telephone shrilled. They both jumped at the sound, and a look of amusement at their shared reaction passed between them.

Aunt Caroline answered it. It didn't take long to figure out from the conversation that it was Ginny on the other end. Norah wondered about the reason for the call, when her mother was supposed to be arriving the next day. After a moment or two, Aunt Caroline handed her the phone and discreetly left the room.

"I'm really sorry, Norah," Ginny began, "but I'm going to have to be out here a little longer. They've got things in a terrible mess."

"But you can't be!" Norah cried. "I'm expecting you here tomorrow!"

"That just isn't possible, dear. I'm still in Victoria. You're okay, aren't you?"

"Of course, I'm okay. But there isn't much to do here, Mother. And all it does is rain."

Ginny laughed her little, bell-like laugh. "You should be used to that, dear! You two are getting along, aren't you? I so much hoped you would."

"Aunt Caroline doesn't really like children, you know," said Norah, in a low voice.

"You're hardly a child, dear," Ginny said. "Can't you try to find little ways to help your aunt? She must have things to do for Christmas."

"I'm trying, Mom, but she doesn't even celebrate Christmas!"

"Really?" The laugh again. "Well, we're going to change that, aren't we? Oh Norah, I'm sorry you're bored, dear. Have you been outside? You took plenty of clothes. Bundle up and get some fresh air. That'll make you feel better."

That afternoon, in sulky solitude, Norah finished the second of the books she'd brought with her.

As the day wore on, the temperature rose, and the freezing rain turned to a misty drizzle. Norah watched from her window as the ice released its hold on the branches and wires, falling to the ground where it shattered. More in an effort to keep awake than taking her mother's suggestion about getting some air, Norah put on her jacket and went out into the backyard late in the day.

Now that the storm was over, the birds were venturing

out from the shelter of the hedge surrounding the property. Norah wished she knew more about birds. She wondered about the name of the little grey ones with the dark eyes, the ones busily picking up all the seed that had fallen from the feeders. She would ask Aunt Caroline. The topic of birds seemed to get the woman talking.

Norah scraped what was left of the ice from the ledges of some of the feeding stations. Four blue jays were picking the seeds out of half-a-dozen sunflower heads laid out on a table in the gazebo. They took flight when Norah approached and screamed at her from the trees nearby. She decided to let them return to their feast. Besides, the wooden steps up into the gazebo didn't look very safe, and she didn't fancy the cold rain off its eaves dripping down the back of her neck.

On the far side of the house and closer to the front was the narrow garage Norah had seen from the taxi. What type of car would an old lady like Aunt Caroline drive, she wondered?

Weeds filled the driveway leading to the garage, and a padlock fastened its wooden, double doors. Standing on tiptoe, Norah peered through the window in a small side door. If Aunt Caroline's car was inside, she couldn't see it in the gloom.

Suddenly, the glass in the window reflected some movement behind her. Norah whirled around, half-expecting to see the strange boy again. It was only Aunt Caroline, out on the front step, shaking dust from a floor mop. Was Norah starting to jump at shadows? But the boy she had seen in the backyard was no shadow. Of that she was sure.

Seven

*J*ody took one step into the backyard of the Stoppard house and spotted the girl at the gazebo, watching the jays. And there, keeping an eye on her from the window in the dining room, was Caroline Stoppard. Immediately, he withdrew to wait behind the hedge.

He'd made up his mind that he had to make a move, do something now. And in order to carry out his plan, he had to get into the house.

It had been years since he had last been inside the Stoppard house. He'd never wanted to frighten Caroline Stoppard. Instead, he'd always kept his distance, content to watch her at work in her garden. After her initial outrage at him trespassing on her property, he felt that she had actually come to accept his silent presence.

When he looked again, Jody saw the girl walk around to the front of the house. Caroline Stoppard was no longer in the window. Moving quickly, he crossed to the back door and crept inside.

It didn't take long to discover a suitcase on the windowsill in one of the upstairs bedrooms at the front of the house. This must be the girl's room, he decided. When he spied the two *books on top of the bookcase by the bed, "Norah B." written inside the front covers, he knew he was right.*

Slipping from the room two minutes later, he nearly ran into the old lady coming up the stairs, her arms filled with clean sheets.

*　　*　　*

Norah walked along the edge of the cedar hedge behind the house. This was where she had seen the boy that morning. There were no footprints visible in the matted grass, as she'd hoped, no bit of cloth caught on the bushes. She stepped through the opening.

On both sides, behind the cedars, lay many flat stones, some still piled on top of each other as if they had once been part of a wall. There was a compost heap here, out of sight of the house and next to that, a pile of brush. Ahead, a path led into the woods. Now that the leaves had fallen from the trees, most of the forest was open to the sky. On a brighter day, it might be a good place for a hike.

Suddenly, Norah saw someone step out of the trees, some distance down the path and stride quickly away in the opposite direction. Even from here, she knew it was the boy again.

"Hey!" she called. "Hey you!" But he was too far away to hear.

That does it! thought Norah. There was nothing wrong with her eyes. It was the same boy all right.

She hurried back to the house. She would try a different approach, but this time she would convince her great-aunt that she wasn't seeing things.

Aunt Caroline was peeling potatoes at the sink when Norah came in through the back door. She kicked off her shoes and carried them across to the boot tray behind the stove. "Do the kids from the neighbourhood ever come here looking for work, Aunt Caroline?" she asked.

"Kids from the neighbourhood?"

"Teenagers, I mean, from Pinegrove maybe? I wondered if any boys from town ever come out here looking for odd jobs."

Aunt Caroline swept the potato peelings into a pail under the sink. "I have a man who mows the grass for me when it gets too high," she said. "In the winter he'll shovel snow if I need him."

"I just wondered if this boy who's hanging around here might be looking for work. I saw him again just now. In the woods out back."

Norah could swear that she saw Aunt Caroline hesitate for a moment, her hands on the edge of the sink, as if she was considering the possibility.

"You know something about him, don't you, Aunt Caroline?" Norah said. "Who is he?"

"He could be anyone," her aunt replied loftily. "My property ends at the hedge."

"He was on that path through the trees," Norah continued. "Right behind this house. Where does that path go, anyway?"

"You used to be able to get to town that way," replied Aunt Caroline. She closed the cupboard and turned to glare at Norah. "Your mother called again after you went outside," she announced. "Seems your cousins are coming tomorrow."

"All right!" Immediately, Norah was aware of her aunt's unsmiling face. "I mean, is that okay with you?"

"Eventually, they'll all arrive, won't they?" Aunt Caroline said. "So it doesn't much matter when."

Norah felt the sudden prickle of perspiration in her palms and under her arms. Her aunt's rudeness always took her by surprise. Surely, the woman realized how hard she was making this visit for both of them.

Aunt Caroline always spoke her mind, with no thought of how it might hurt someone's feelings. Now Norah decided it was her turn to speak up. She clenched her hands behind her back, confident that the worst that could happen would be that she'd be sent packing.

"Aunt Caroline, it's not hard to tell that you don't like me being here." She swallowed, her pulse pounding in her ears. "I'm really sorry that Mom dumped me off on you like this. She shouldn't have. It was sort of, of…" She ran out of words.

"Presumptuous?" Aunt Caroline offered, one eyebrow raised.

"Yes, I guess so. She shouldn't have figured just because we were related that you'd want us here. But that's the way Mom is. I can't do much about it, now that I *am* here. Mom was just so happy to find out about you, she figured you'd feel the same way about us. I can see now that she was wrong. If there was any way that I could leave, I would."

There, she'd said it. Now it was Aunt Caroline's turn.

For what seemed like a long time, Great-aunt Caroline

did not say anything, although Norah thought she detected a softening around her mouth. She held her breath. It wouldn't take her long to zip up her suitcase and be out of there.

"You have more spunk than I gave you credit for," the woman said, at last.

"Were you testing me, or something?"

"No. Well, maybe I was. Anyway, I can see you are the sensible one in your family." Caroline Stoppard's tone was less bitter than Norah had come to expect.

She shrugged, felt her shoulders suddenly relax. "It's just that my mom is the kind of person who is always sure everything will work out for the best. It's kind of her motto."

"Her name's not Pollyanna, is it?" Aunt Caroline asked in a wry tone.

"No, it's Ginny. Why do you ask that?"

"Oh, Pollyanna's just a character in American literature, the eternal optimist." There was a hint of a smile now on the woman's face. "Never mind, Norah," she said with a sigh. "You're right; it's not your fault. I should have realized that; I'm the adult here. It's going to take me a while to get used to having people in this house, but I expect we'll all survive this visit. Then everything can get back to normal again."

"We could do better than just survive," Norah ventured, "if we all tried to get along."

But the smile had disappeared again as quickly as it had come. Norah knew Aunt Caroline's words were as close to an apology as she was likely to get. Would things between them be any better now, she wondered?

"When you go upstairs," the woman said, "you'll see that I've made up the room at the top of the stairs for your cousin Andrew. It used to be the nursery."

"I don't think we should tell him that," Norah suggested. The fact that Norah was teasing seemed lost on her great-aunt. "Suit yourself," Aunt Caroline said. "I put him there because the other rooms are larger, and he's the only one having a room to himself. The girl can share a bed with you, until your mother comes."

"They're good kids," Norah promised, "Becca and Andrew. You'll see."

"Well, I expect you'll all be able to entertain yourselves," declared Aunt Caroline, and she turned back to the vegetables waiting in the sink.

* * *

Jody put his knee on a length of board to steady it and picked up the handsaw. Again and again that evening, he found his thoughts returning to the girl.

Her name was Norah. Norah B. She'd seen him too, on the path, and she'd called out to him. Why hadn't he turned around? What was the matter with him? He'd let the opportunity to talk to her slip by. It had been a long time since he'd spoken to anyone from the big house. Not since Joseph.

Blowing sawdust off the section he'd cut, Jody began to sand the wood smooth. With each stroke, he became more determined that the next time would be different. He would have to watch the house more closely now, and the very next opportunity he got to approach the girl, he would do it!

Eight

As she stood in a puddle of warm sunlight to pull on her clothes the next morning, Norah felt she might have dreamed the horrible weather of the day before. Today looked to be the exact opposite. She was counting the hours until Becca and Andrew arrived.

She was making her bed when she discovered the box with the Christmas present she had bought for her mother, shoved under one of the pillows. It was a delicate blue scarf, with rivers of turquoise and green running though the silky material. She had known the moment she saw it that it was the perfect gift for Ginny. She'd been hiding it since October.

Seeing as Becca would be sharing the bed after today, Norah tucked the box into the top drawer of the bureau. Ginny would be bringing the rest of the presents with her, but now Norah wished she had thought to buy something special to give to Becca, something she had picked out herself, like the scarf. Maybe there was still time.

In spite of her resolve to get up early, Norah did not make it to the dining room before her great-aunt had finished breakfast. The thump, thump of a washing machine in the basement revealed the woman's whereabouts.

Norah broke open a box of cereal flakes and thought about the day ahead. The cousins would be arriving on the afternoon train, so there'd be enough time to walk to town this morning to see if she could find that gift for Becca.

Clearing away her breakfast things, she fetched her jacket from the front hall. "I'm going out, Aunt Caroline," she called from the top of the basement stairs. The only reply was the squeal of the old-fashioned wringer.

Norah descended three steps into the gloom. "Is that okay? I thought I'd walk back to the town. I still have some Christmas shopping to do."

In the light of the single bulb that dangled from a beam overhead, Aunt Caroline guided a bed sheet through the wringer, squeezing all the water out before it dropped into a basket on the floor. "It's a fair walk," the woman commented, without looking up. "The number for the taxi is by the phone."

"I'd really rather walk," Norah told her. "It's nice and sunny out."

"Suit yourself. You walk facing the traffic, remember?"

"I know that, Aunt Caroline."

"Well, you aren't used to walking along the roadside. There are no sidewalks here in the country."

Not about to waste any more time arguing, Norah backed up the stairs. "I won't stay long," she promised. "I'll be back in time for lunch."

She hesitated on the back step, looking towards the

opening in the hedge and the path through the trees. Why follow the highway, when there was a way to get to town, practically in the backyard?

Norah crossed to the hedge. Sunlight danced on the path, beckoning her. Pinegrove couldn't be very far. It had taken the taxi only a few minutes to come by the highway. She stepped out with confidence, putting any idea about losing her way to the back of her mind. Aunt Caroline had said the path led into town. How could anyone get lost over such a short distance?

As Norah got deeper into the woods, she found the path slippery with wet leaves, even muddy in places from all the rain. She had been walking about ten minutes when she came to a place where a number of trees had fallen across the path. The ground underfoot was becoming soggier with every step. Eventually, she put one foot down into water so deep it went over the top of her sneaker. The path had come to an abrupt end.

Directly in front of her was a large pond, sprouting clumps of cattails here and there. Fallen trees covered much of its surface. Norah could see a skin of ice at the edge of the brackish water. Had she left the path some ways back, without knowing it?

Sure she that she would arrive back on the path she'd been following, Norah retraced her steps. Instead, heavy underbrush crowded her route. Where had she gotten turned around?

She trekked back again to the edge of the pond. There had to be a way to get around this obstacle. But where to pick up the path again?

Norah sat down on a fallen log to consider what to do. If she sat right there in one place, as she'd heard you were supposed to when you were lost, how long would it be before Aunt Caroline sent someone to look for her? But she wasn't lost! And anyway, Aunt Caroline would not send someone into the woods. She would assume Norah was walking to town along the road. Which was what she should have been doing.

Norah fought the feeling of rising panic, willing herself to sit for five minutes and take deep breaths. It was early in the day. Someone was sure to come along before it got dark. Or should she try walking in the other direction?

She was bending down to retie the muddy laces on her sneakers when, all at once, she heard the sound of someone whistling. A passerby already!

Norah leapt to her feet, giddy with relief. And there, from out of the trees behind her, strode the boy she'd seen at Aunt Caroline's.

"Hi there," he greeted her, running his hands through thick, brown hair that immediately flopped again over his forehead. "Nice day, isn't it?" A lopsided grin revealed slightly crooked teeth. His complexion was clear, with a smattering of freckles and the shadow of darker hair above his lip.

"Nice," Norah agreed. "Unless you happen to be lost, which I think I might be."

"Where were you going?"

"Into Pinegrove," replied Norah. "I thought this was the way, but I lost the path I was following."

"I know what you mean. Path's pretty easy to follow till you get to this point," the boy agreed. "But if you keep to the left you'll be on it again. Come on. I'll show you." He smiled again. "My name's Jody, by the way. And since we're both headed in the same direction we might as well walk together. Okay with you? It's Norah, isn't it?"

"That's right," said Norah, wondering who could have told him that.

"And your last name?" he queried. "Is it Brown, or Bailey? Blake, maybe."

"It's Bingham," said Norah.

"Right. Norah Bingham. Just watch where you step then, Norah Bingham, and follow me."

Nine

The boy was a little taller than Norah and very thin. The skinny legs of the khaki pants he wore made him look even more like a toothpick. There was something peculiar about his clothing. The short, brown jacket made of corduroy was open, and underneath he wore a green shirt with black stripes, tightly buttoned at the neck. The points of the narrow shirt collar were also buttoned down. Instead of sneakers, he was wearing brown, leather dress shoes, and they looked a little the worse for all the rain. The retro look, Norah decided. Outfits from the sixties were big back home too.

"This used to be just a creek through here," Jody was saying. "All you had to do in the old days was jump across. But the beavers have dammed it up, so now it's more like a lake."

"The beavers did all this?" Norah marvelled. Everywhere she looked there were three-foot stumps, their tops gnawed off to rough points.

"A whole team of them," Jody acknowledged. "You can see their lodges. There's one there." He pointed to an untidy mound of sticks and mud at the end of the pond.

"This part of the woods has really changed since the last time I was here," he said.

Norah watched him out of the corner of her eye, thinking that he talked as if he were a real old-timer. They continued together on to drier ground. "Haven't I seen you hanging around the Stoppard house?" she challenged.

"You might have," Jody said agreeably.

"Oh, I'm sure that I did," she said. "Why didn't you just come knock on the door, if you wanted something?"

"I didn't want anything," he said. "I was just passing by."

"It looked more like you were spying on us," declared Norah.

"I'm not spying! I'm staying in these parts for a while. I pass the house whenever I take this shortcut to town."

"Where exactly are you staying?" she asked.

"Oh, here and there," Jody replied.

Norah stopped in her tracks. "What kind of an answer is that?" she demanded.

Jody laughed. "Not a very good one, I guess." He started walking backwards until she caught up again. "Are you visiting Miss Stoppard now?"

"I'm here for Christmas. Today more of the family is coming."

"The family?" he asked. "I didn't think the old lady had much family."

"She doesn't. The cousins are on my mother's side."

"Not Binghams, then," Jody stated.

"No, they're Moores."

"But you're a relative?" he asked.

"Miss Stoppard is my great-aunt, my father's aunt.

46

Dad's mother was Agnes Stoppard, Caroline's sister. She's dead, and so is my dad. So there's just Mom and me." Norah narrowed her eyes at him. "You deny then that you were watching Aunt Caroline?"

Jody threw up his hands. "I swear. I don't mean Miss Stoppard any harm. Far from it."

"Well, I think I'd better warn you anyway," Norah said. "If she thinks you're lurking around, my bet is she'll call the police."

Jody nodded, looking solemn again. "I wouldn't like to think she would," he said. "But she's older now, so you might be right." He said nothing more for a few moments. Then, "Did she tell you she used to run the library in town?"

"She never mentioned it," Norah realized. "But we really don't talk much."

"Well, she's likely retired by now. But she was a librarian practically her whole life. Just like her father was all his life."

"How do you know so much about them?" Norah asked. "You're just a kid."

"Fifteen," he protested. "But my family's from these parts. There's a bed ready for me here whenever I come."

By this time, the two had left the trees behind and started across a field stubbled with corn stalks. "We just drop down to the left here," Jody explained, "till we get to a fence and carry on along the edge of the field a ways. You'll see."

"Listen," Norah said, panting a little as she kept pace with him over the rough ground. "How did you know my name?"

47

"This is a pretty small place," Jody said. "You'll find everyone knows everyone else's business around here."

Remembering the taxi driver's comments, Norah knew that was probably true. "The cabbie who brought me from the station the other day called Aunt Caroline a recluse," she said.

"That sounds about right. She hardly ever goes anywhere now, and no one comes to visit her."

Norah was still thinking he knew an awful lot about what went on in the Stoppard house, when Jody unexpectedly stopped. "Well, this is my street," he announced. "I'm going up this way to the lumberyard."

"Are you building something?" Norah asked.

"From time to time I am. The people at the lumberyard don't mind if I rummage around, take bits and pieces that they can't sell."

"So, what do you do with all the bits and pieces?"

"I make things, little doo-dads, to give to my friends." He raised an arm to point to the left. "Okay, the main street's straight ahead there," he directed. "You'll come to the sidewalk soon. This is where I leave you. 'Bye for now." And with that, he turned and headed up the street.

"Hey, wait a sec," Norah cried, running to catch up with him. "I'm actually going this way myself." Although until that moment, she'd had no idea that she was. "I'm looking for a Christmas present for my cousin," she explained. There was a sign across the front of the lumber store indicating that the place sold hardware and sundries.

"Good luck, then," said Jody.

Behind the main building there was a row of open,

metal sheds and beyond that, several piles of logs waiting to be planed. Assuming that he would use the same entrance she would, Norah was startled when Jody suddenly left her side and hopped over the fence. She stood there gaping as he strolled casually away across the lumberyard, his fingers in the front pockets of his skinny pants, the jacket billowing out behind him.

Ten

When Norah entered the store at the front of the lumberyard, every head in the place turned to look at her. A man carrying a yellow bag of sidewalk salt on his shoulder had to make a deliberate little circle in order to see her around the bag.

At the back of the store, Norah found a section selling kitchen supplies—gadgets to sliver cheese, ice trays that would turn out cubes the shape of hearts and diamonds, but nothing for a ten-year-old girl. "Merry Christmas," she murmured to the clerk at the checkout, with an apologetic smile. She left the store, feeling all eyes on her back.

Retracing her steps, Norah returned to the main street. From the fried chicken shop on the one corner, she could see the whole town. She walked its single block to the western end, where there was a garage with one gas pump. The attendant sat in the unexpected warmth of the December sun, his chair tilted on its back legs against the front of the building. Spotting Norah, he immediately brought the chair back down onto its four legs.

Halfway back down the block, there was a variety store that sold bread and milk and lottery tickets. A repair truck was pulled up to the curb, the yellow light on its roof revolving slowly.

While Norah stood and read the signs of coming events that plastered the windows of the store, she stole a look inside. Three men in work clothes hunched on stools over mugs of coffee. The counter was bare, except for a plate of muffins covered by a glass dome. It didn't seem a likely place to find a Christmas present.

Across the road there was a drug store that doubled as the post office. Maybe at the very least, Norah thought, she could find some hair barrettes or some bath beads in the drug store. She crossed over and entered the shop.

With the exception of a woman knitting behind the counter, the place was deserted. The store was so quiet she could hear the click, click of the knitting needles.

A sign suspended from the ceiling pointed the way to a small gift section at the back. Perusing its glass shelves one by one, Norah was delighted to find at last the perfect gift for Becca. It was a miniature bird with a pinkish breast, nestled in a tiny, grapevine wreath. She picked it up and stroked the bird's velvety back.

"This is just what I was looking for," she told the woman at the counter, unsnapping her wallet.

"Then I'm very glad you came in," the storekeeper said. She set aside the knitting and, ringing up the sale, rolled the gift in tissue paper before placing it into a plastic bag. "You're at Miss Stoppard's, aren't you?"

"Why, yes," said Norah. But she was not really surprised at the question.

"Caroline Stoppard doesn't get much company,"

observed the woman. She handed Norah the bag.

"So I've heard," said Norah. And because she didn't want to appear unfriendly, she asked, "The kids who live in this town, where do they go to school?"

"Over to Hanley. School bus takes them. It's about a half-hour down the highway, you know. There's a mall over to Hanley." The woman's tone was sorrowful. "That's where everyone shops now."

Norah hesitated before opening the door to the shop again. "Can you tell me where the library is?" she inquired.

"There's a big library in Hanley," the shopkeeper replied. Then, "Oh, you mean Miss Stoppard's library." She came out from behind the counter and beckoned Norah over to the front window. "See that little building across the street?"

The sign over the door of a small, frame structure on the other side of the road read: New To U Clothing. Consignments Welcome. "That's where the library used to be."

Norah frowned. "Used to be?"

"Just after Caroline Stoppard retired, it closed, and everything was moved to Hanley."

It struck Norah how disappointed Aunt Caroline must have been at that outcome. "That's too bad," she said.

The woman returned to her cash register. "It sure is," she said, with feeling. "Especially after a person puts her whole life into trying to keep something open."

The shopkeeper had resumed her knitting, and Norah gently pulled the door shut behind her. Checking her watch, she saw she'd have to hurry to be back to Aunt Caroline's by noon. She had already decided there would be no shortcuts; she would follow the highway home.

Norah headed down the street, relieved to be leaving the dreary little town. Clearly, no one in Pinegrove had much excitement in his or her life. If her visit had been the big news of the day, what would the citizens have thought if they had seen the boy who had hopped the fence at the lumberyard?

It was only then that Norah realized Jody had never told her where he was staying. Instead, he had switched the questions around so that she was telling him what he wanted to know.

*   *   *

Jody grinned with satisfaction. This had been his lucky day, all right! Not only had he discovered a big pile of bark for the taking at the lumberyard—long strips planed off the rough boards—but he'd actually talked to the girl.

Norah Bingham. The grin grew wider. He wondered what her reaction would have been, had he told her they shared the same last name.

Arms filled with every bit that he could carry, Jody took the path back to the shed in the woods.

*   *   *

Aunt Caroline was stirring a pot of something on the stove when Norah came in through the back door. The woman looked up briefly and remarked, "That didn't take you long."

"Not much happening in Pinegrove," Norah said. She slid off her sneakers without untying them and shrugged out of her jacket. "The woman in the drugstore said everyone shops at the mall in Hanley. Do you ever go there?"

"Never. And I don't intend to."

"Don't you go anywhere, Aunt Caroline? The taxi driver told me you have a car."

"*Had* a car," her great-aunt snorted. "That's how much he knows. I sold it last spring."

Aunt Caroline tapped the wooden spoon against the edge of the pot and set it to one side. "Of course I go out, if I have a medical appointment or something important. But I loathe shopping malls, and I don't go into Pinegrove either. That way I don't give them anything to talk about."

"You think people talk about you behind your back?" Norah was puzzled. "What would they say?"

"Who knows?"

"I think you're wrong about the people, Aunt Caroline. I think they're just interested in you."

"And why would that be, now?"

"Well, you ran the library in Pinegrove, didn't you?"

"My, my. They have been doing some talking."

"Well, if you went to work in town every day for years and years, and then after you retired the people never saw you again, they must wonder if you're okay. That you haven't *died* or something."

Aunt Caroline gave an indignant sniff and reached for the paprika.

Norah persisted. "Aren't you the least bit interested in what goes on in town?"

"I know what goes on, whether I want to or not. The grocery man always finds a way to sneak the local paper into my shopping bag. I don't ask him for it, so I make sure it goes right back the next time." She slammed the door of the spice cupboard.

"You see, Aunt Caroline, people *do* care about you! If he gives you a free paper…"

"Why are we having this conversation, Norah?" Her great-aunt turned from the stove, her hands on her hips. "If you're still so determined to be of help, please set the table for our lunch."

"First, can I show you what I got for Becca?" Norah asked meekly, taking the gift from the plastic bag. "The reason I went into town in the first place. There, isn't he cute?"

Aunt Caroline stepped away, the better to see through the bottom of her glasses what Norah was holding in the palm of her hand.

When Caroline Stoppard spied the little bird in its grapevine nest, Norah witnessed a transformation in the woman's face. There were smile wrinkles around the eyes and the usually bitter mouth.

Aunt Caroline reached out a finger and gently touched the red patch on the little creature's head. "It's a redpoll," she said, her voice tender. "Tiny, but very hardy little fellows. They love the winter, you know: the colder the better. But they leave us when summer comes."

"I should have bought you one too, Aunt Caroline!" Norah suddenly realized.

"Not when I have the real thing," her aunt said, picking up the wooden spoon and turning back to the stove.

Eleven

Norah watched from her bedroom window until she saw the yellow taxi turn into the lane. Hurrying downstairs, she waited till she heard her cousins' voices on the other side of the front door, before yanking it open. "Surprise!"

"Hey! What took you so long?" demanded Andrew, his hand raised to lift the knocker. He recovered quickly and slung his pack across the threshold. Becca bobbed up and down behind him. "You scared us, Norah," she exclaimed happily.

Norah drew the little girl inside and wrapped her in an enormous hug, backpack and all. "Becca, I'm so glad to see you!"

"Let's skip the hugs, okay?" said Andrew, closing the door behind him. He took a minute to look around. "Awesome!" he decided. "I kind of expected some creepy servant to answer the door. This place is right out of a horror movie."

"I know," Norah agreed. "But the very first thing Aunt Caroline told me was that there were no servants here, creepy or otherwise."

She studied her fair-haired cousins while they took off their shoes and unzipped their jackets. If it was possible, Andrew had even more freckles than the last time she'd seen him, and he'd grown three inches at least. He was as tall and thin as Becca was short and sturdy.

"Where is your great-aunt?" the little girl inquired, unwinding her scarf, her round cheeks flushed with excitement.

"She's around here somewhere," Norah said, shrugging. "In this big house, we lose each other pretty easily. Here, I'll show you where you can hang those jackets."

Suddenly, the door under the stairs that led to the basement flew open, and Aunt Caroline appeared with an armload of firewood. Andrew immediately sprang forward. "Let me help you with that!" he cried.

"I've come this far with it," snapped Aunt Caroline, brushing him off. "I'm sure I can cross the hall without dropping it."

The children exchanged startled glances. "These are my cousins, Aunt Caroline," Norah announced, trailing the woman into the den and indicating that the others were to follow. "This is Andrew, and this is Rebecca. But everyone just calls her Becca." She put a protective arm around the little girl's shoulders. Caroline Stoppard's sour attitude was not going to spoil her own happiness at having her cousins for company.

Aunt Caroline set the wood down onto the hearth and turned to examine the children. "Well, she'll be Rebecca while she's here," she declared. "Never did understand why people had to go shortening up perfectly respectable names." She glowered at Andrew. "And I suppose they call you Andy," she said.

"Hardly anyone does," he protested.

"Aunt Caroline," Becca chirped bravely. "Thank you for inviting us to spend Christmas with you."

The woman fixed her with a steely-eyed gaze. "Well, as I'm sure Norah will tell you, it wasn't exactly my idea." She bent to arrange some small pieces of wood in the fireplace and reached for a box of matches on the mantle. Striking one, she held it to the wad of paper she had stuffed in amongst the sticks. Everyone waited for the kindling to catch the flame.

"There now," Aunt Caroline announced, brushing her hands together, "that should take the chill off." And then, as if surprised to find the children still standing there, "Well Norah, where are your manners? Aren't you going to show your cousins to their rooms, let them get settled in?"

Meekly, brother and sister followed Norah up the stairs to the second floor. "Don't let Aunt Caroline bother you," Norah advised, once she had opened the door to her room and they were all safely inside. "You know the saying about someone's bark being worse than their bite? That's the way it is with her."

"She *is* pretty scary," Becca said, making a face.

"Not once you get to know her. She lit that fire down there for you, you know."

"She did?"

"Absolutely. Now, this is our room, Becca, and yours is next door, Andrew." Norah set Becca's backpack on the big bed, before returning to the hall to open the door of the room on the right. "It's a little smaller than ours," she said, "but you have it all to yourself."

"Holy! Why's it so cold in here?" Andrew asked, dropping his pack and hugging himself. "I hope she doesn't expect that fire in the den to heat the whole house. Doesn't she have a furnace?"

"She has a furnace. She just doesn't like to use it," Norah explained. "But the kitchen is always warm. There's a wood stove in there, and that's where I spend most of my time. Aunt Caroline isn't used to having other people around, but I've learned that if I am quiet, she puts up with me."

"What do you mean, she puts up with you?" Becca sounded bewildered. "Isn't she happy that you're here?"

"I think I was a bit of a surprise to her," Norah admitted, hiking herself up to sit on the edge of Andrew's bed. "She probably didn't know she had any relatives, and then we all start showing up at once."

"Well, I'm sure once she gets to know us, she'll like us," said Becca, with confidence.

"It's not that she doesn't like us, Becca," Norah pointed out. "She's an old lady, not used to children. But she's coming around. She really is."

Andrew began emptying the contents of his pack on the bed and sorting through the clothing. "I'm glad to see you've brought some sweatshirts," Norah remarked. "You'll need them here." She scanned the room. "I guess there isn't a dresser here for you to put your clothes in."

"Why can't he just use this closet?" Becca suggested, twisting the knob on a door in the wall. "Oh, I guess not. It seems to be locked."

"Doesn't matter," said Andrew. "My things don't need to be hung up anyway. I brought mostly jeans and sweats."

Norah tried the closet door for herself. "I guess she has something in there she doesn't want us to see. Funny that she'd lock it."

"This is what I was looking for!" Andrew announced, pulling a square, blue box from the tangle on the bed. He lifted the flaps and took out a snow globe. "Becca and I brought this for Aunt Caroline." He held it up for Norah. "What do you think?"

Inside the glass globe, a family was dragging an evergreen tree from the forest towards a house with lighted windows, a black and white dog bounding at their heels. "It's beautiful," Norah said, turning it upside-down and letting snowflakes drift over the scene. "Just the way Christmas should be."

"It's not a Christmas present," Becca explained. "It's a thank-you-for-having-us gift. Let's give it to her right now. I'm sure it'll cheer her up."

"I think we should wait for just the right moment," her brother advised and began stuffing his clothes back into the pack. He ignored the pout that had formed on Becca's face. "Found anything interesting to do around here yet, Norah?"

"This is the first day it hasn't rained," Norah admitted. "But I'm dying to tell you what happened this morning."

She resumed her perch on the edge of the bed. "Aunt Caroline doesn't know it yet, but I got lost in the woods this morning."

"You did?" Becca's look turned worried. "How did you get back here again?"

"What were you doing in the woods?" demanded Andrew.

"Aunt Caroline told me you used to be able to get to Pinegrove if you followed the path out back. But listen! There's this boy. His name is Jody. I've seen him hanging around here a couple of times."

Andrew frowned. "Hanging around?"

"Well, he doesn't do much except watch us. Anyway, just after I found I'd gotten off the path this morning and was wondering how I was going to find my way out of the woods, he showed up. Talk about perfect timing! He was going to the village too, so he said he'd show me the way."

"You were really lucky he came along, then," declared Andrew. "You shouldn't go walking in strange places all by yourself, especially not in the woods."

"I know." Norah sighed resignedly and got to her feet. "I came back from town by myself, along the road." She slid off the bed then and looked at her watch. "There's time to go and look around outside for a while, if you want to. Supper is at six sharp, and Aunt Caroline doesn't like dawdlers."

Twelve

B efore the girls returned to the room they would be sharing, Norah pointed out the other doors along the hall. "That's got to be Aunt Caroline's room," she said, indicating the closed door next to Andrew's, at the end of the hall. "There's an empty bedroom on the other side of ours. The bathroom and a room she uses for storage are there, across the hall. Come on, I'll show you."

Norah leaned in closer to the little girl. "Guess what she keeps in this room, Becca? There's a woman in here with no head!"

Becca clapped a hand over her mouth in horror.

Laughing at the reaction, Norah explained. "It's just a dressmaker's form, Bec—a woman with a very small waist and no head. I was teasing you. Come on; I heard Andrew go downstairs already."

On the landing of the stairs, Norah put out a hand to restrain Becca a moment. "Now here's something really weird," she said in a low voice. "Have you noticed how there are no pictures on any of these walls?"

The little girl looked around at the stairway and down into the vast entrance below. "I haven't actually seen the whole house yet," she admitted.

"No, but you will," Norah promised. They reached the bottom, and she handed Becca her jacket off the hallstand, then retrieved her own. "You'll see there are no paintings or anything, anywhere in the house."

Becca pulled her scarf out of the sleeve of her jacket and hung it back on the hook. "Maybe Great-aunt Caroline doesn't like art," she suggested.

"There's all kinds of it up in the spare room," said Norah. "Not on the walls, but standing on the floor, stacked one against the other. Oil paintings, in frames. So they must have hung on the walls here once. You know what Aunt Caroline told me? That she didn't have any use for such things now."

"That *is* weird," Becca agreed.

Coming out onto the back step, the girls could see Andrew in the gazebo. He was examining the sunflower heads spread out on the table there. "Man, the size of these things!" he exclaimed as the girls approached. "I wonder if she grows them herself?"

"She does," Norah told him, waiting for Becca to catch up.

The array of birdfeeders in the yard had captured Becca's attention. "Look at them all," she cried, spinning around. "They're everywhere! Why does she have so many?"

"Because every bird in the neighbourhood comes here to be fed. It's a hobby of hers," Norah explained. "See the little birds that eat the seed off the ground? They're juncos, Aunt Caroline told me. And those birds that dip and dive between the feeders, like they're on a roller coaster?"

"I already know what they are," Becca said. "They're chickadees."

Norah nodded. "There are some really pretty birds coming to the feeders. You should watch for the cardinals, Becca—they're the red ones. They like to eat by themselves, so you mostly see them first thing in the morning or later in the day. The feathers on their heads stick up, like they're wearing little hats. Aunt Caroline can even imitate their song. They don't sing much in the winter, though."

"You know what, Norah?" Becca's round face was suddenly serious. "Anyone who feeds the birds has to be a nice person."

"Aunt Caroline is a nice person," Norah said. "But she does seem to have a lot of secrets. And sometimes it's like she doesn't want anyone to know she's a nice person. I stood up to her the other day and saw another side of her."

"That was awfully brave of you," remarked Becca.

"She told me she was having a hard time getting used to having me here."

Andrew had climbed up onto the gazebo railing to survey the view from there. "I can see the woods out behind," he announced. "And the path you must have taken, Norah."

"I wouldn't stand up there if I were you," Norah advised. "The railing is kind of old and rickety."

A sudden flash of movement caught her eye. "Oh, look over there! I'll bet it's that boy again."

"Where?" Andrew demanded. "I don't see anyone."

"No, he's gone now. Every time I've seen him, he's

either standing in the yard or going through the woods. And up until this morning, he would disappear almost as soon as I saw him."

"No kidding?" from Andrew.

"I think he's watching the house," said Norah. The others were staring wide-eyed at her now. "He says he isn't," she went on. "But I've seen him every day since I got here, just standing there, watching us."

Three pairs of eyes automatically shifted back to the house, trying to see what anyone spying on it would see. In the light of the kitchen, Aunt Caroline was moving about, getting supper ready, oblivious to the children watching her from the yard.

"Norah, you're scaring me," said Becca, shuffling closer to her.

Norah was quick to reassure her. "He's not scary any more, now that I've met him. His name is Jody, and he's just an ordinary kid. But it's like, I can't figure out where he comes from. He just sort of appears. I look out the window and there he is."

"Do you suppose he's got a hideout or something built in the woods?" Andrew suggested, jumping down from his perch. "Somewhere he can get to in a hurry?"

"I don't know. Why would you ask that?"

"Well, if he lived in the neighbourhood, you'd think you'd see him out front, wouldn't you?"

"I guess," said Norah. "I asked him where he was staying, but he gave me the strangest answer. He said his family was from these parts, that he was staying here and there. I figure he must be visiting his relatives. But he managed to avoid telling me where exactly."

"On purpose?" Andrew wondered. He lowered himself onto the top step of the gazebo where the girls now sat. "Do you think he doesn't want you to know?"

"I don't know," Norah said again. "He's just the strangest boy I've ever met. I figured I was lost, and he comes out of the trees and offers to show me the way, like we'd been friends all along.

"He was going to the lumberyard to get some pieces of wood, said that he could have whatever they were throwing out. But I'm not sure the people in the village know what he's up to."

Andrew frowned. "You mean, you think he's stealing?"

"No," Norah said slowly, "I don't think the people even know that he's there."

"Then he is stealing," Becca declared.

"Well, he didn't try to hide or anything, but instead of using the front door of the store like everyone else, he jumped over the fence." Norah looked up again at the kitchen window. "The weirdest thing is that every time I mention him to Aunt Caroline, she doesn't seem to believe me."

"Why not?"

"Who knows? She just keeps changing the subject whenever I say I've seen him. I get the feeling there's something she's not telling me. Like she doesn't want to know he's out here."

By this time, Becca had moved so close to Norah on the step that she was almost sitting in her lap. "Maybe we should be going in now," Norah suggested, looking down at her young cousin. "We don't want to be late for supper."

Becca didn't need any encouragement. She gave one last look over her shoulder at the woods where night had fallen and was the first one to the door.

The table in the dining room was set for four when they passed through on the way to clean up for supper. "You know what?" Becca asked. "I'm going to get that present for Aunt Caroline right now. And no arguments from you, Mister Bossy Andrew!"

A few minutes later, she put the snow globe in the centre of the place mat at the head of the table. The children took their seats.

Aunt Caroline came out of the kitchen. "Macaroni and cheese," she announced grimly and set a casserole down in front of them.

"One of my favourites," declared Andrew, shaking out the napkin he'd taken from beside his plate and tucking it into the neck of his sweatshirt.

"That napkin goes into your lap until you need it," Aunt Caroline instructed. She scowled at the snow globe in front of her. "What's this now?" she demanded.

"A thank-you gift," said Becca, beaming. "To say thank you for having us."

"Entirely unnecessary," declared Aunt Caroline and set the gift to one side.

"Turn it upside-down," Andrew invited. "It's really nice when it snows."

Aunt Caroline ignored the suggestion and thrust the basket of dinner rolls under his nose.

They ate in silence, stealing looks at one another only when they dared.

"We can help you get ready for Christmas," Andrew offered, between courses. "Put up your decorations."

"If I had such things." Aunt Caroline stiffened at the suggestion. She rose to clear the plates.

Andrew looked quickly at Norah. "Oh well, never mind. Mom and Dad and Aunt Ginny are bringing everything. Even a tree, since Aunt Ginny said you didn't have one yet. Dad said he'd have to tie it to the top of the van, but we'll have a tree."

"And presents," breathed Becca, her blue eyes sparkling. "Lots and lots of presents."

"Such frivolity," muttered the old lady. But before she pushed through the kitchen door, they saw the ghost of a smile pass over her lips.

Thirteen

Jody slipped away from the house again and into the trees, worry nagging at him. Norah had told him the cousins were coming, and now he'd seen them for himself—a boy about his own age, he figured, and a younger girl with curly, yellow hair. The fact that the children were already here meant the adults couldn't be far behind. Before he knew it, Christmas would be over, and Norah Bingham would be gone. Would she find what he had hidden in time to make a difference?

*   *   *

With supper finished and Aunt Caroline refusing all offers of help, the cousins regrouped in the den. "Another fun-filled meal at Caroline Stoppard's," remarked Norah, dropping into the leather sofa. The fire had gone out.

"You know what I think?" Becca began. "I think that no one has given your Great-aunt Caroline a present in years. No wonder she's unhappy. But did you see? She smiled. Kind of."

"You could be right," Norah agreed. "But when she's

so prickly, can you blame them? She never lets anyone get close to her. I learned more about Aunt Caroline from one trip to town today than I ever learned from her."

Andrew yawned, stretching long arms over his head. "I've got a feeling it's going to take more than a Christmas tree and presents to cheer this place up," he said. "I think I'll just go on up to my room."

"But it's still early!" Becca protested. "If your aunt has some cards, Norah, maybe we could play Crazy Eights or something."

"Not tonight, Becca," Andrew said and left the room.

"You're no fun," declared his sister. She turned down the corners of her mouth at Andrew's back.

"We might as well go up too, Becca," Norah said. "You still have to unpack."

No sooner had the girls reached the top of the stairs than, to Norah's surprise, Becca skipped over to Aunt Caroline's door at the end of the hall. With a finger to her lips, Becca turned the knob and opened it. The door swung wide on its hinges.

"Becca!" Norah whispered hoarsely. "What're you doing?"

"Just taking a look," said Becca, a mischievous gleam in her eye. "Don't tell me you aren't curious."

Admittedly intrigued, Norah took a step toward the doorway. Becca was already inside.

The single light in the hall behind them barely illuminated a large bedroom with windows on three sides. Norah saw a writing desk and two dressers made of dark wood, polished to a high sheen. An oval mirror hung above one of the dressers, and a low stool was drawn up to it. Centred on the wall to the right of the door was a narrow bed, smoothly made up with a snowy white bedspread. Three armchairs were placed in an alcove under the windows at the end of the room, a round coffee table in front.

It was a fine bedroom, but it looked to Norah as if the owner spent little time in it; everything was in such perfect order. There was not a newspaper or an empty teacup in sight. Through a partially open door in one corner of the room, Norah glimpsed the white fixtures of an en suite bathroom.

There was also a door in the left wall, a large key in the lock. "I think this goes into Andrew's room, don't you?" whispered Becca, crossing over to it. Norah realized that it was possible that the two rooms were connected, since Aunt Caroline had said the smaller room was once the nursery.

But something else had caught Norah's attention. There was a single photograph, its loose edges curling, tucked into the frame of the mirror over the dressing table. With a quick glance over her shoulder, Norah tiptoed over for a closer look. In the dim light, she could make out a small child dressed in a cowboy outfit and perched on a spotted pony. Someone out of camera range was holding the reins of the animal.

Becca came up beside her. "I wonder who that is."

"Could be anyone, I guess," said Norah. "It could even be my father. Aunt Caroline said they'd never met, but her sister may have sent her a picture of him."

Becca frowned. "Do you think it's a boy?"

"Well, in the old days, little boys sometimes had long curls. But maybe it's Aunt Caroline herself."

"It must be someone special, anyway," Becca decided. "It's the only picture she's got in her room. Here, why don't we turn on this lamp so we can see it better."

"No, Becca!" Norah snatched her cousin's hand, preventing her from turning the switch.

At that very instant, they heard someone coming up the stairs towards them. With one panicked look into each other's eyes, they darted for the only escape.

"This way!" Norah choked, lunging towards the door in the wall. Swiftly, she turned the key. They both dove through, and Norah pulled the door shut behind them.

They were in Andrew's room.

"I was right!" gasped Becca. "It wasn't a closet."

Andrew had been lying, fully clothed, on his bed, arms folded behind his head. He leapt to his feet when the girls burst through the door. "Holy cow! Where'd you come from?" he croaked.

"Ssh!" The girls pressed their backs against the wall. "It's Aunt Caroline!" Then, to her horror, Norah realized that she still clutched in her hand the key to the door.

"What were you doing in there?" Andrew demanded.

"Nothing," said his sister. "Just looking. We didn't touch anything." She looked to Norah for moral support. "We weren't even sure whose room it was, were we, Norah? And then we heard her coming upstairs."

Andrew shook his head in disbelief and sat down again on the edge of the bed. Norah slid up to sit beside him. Slowly, she opened her hand to show the others what she had brought with her.

"Oh, no!" Becca gulped. "What'll we do now?"

Norah did the only thing she could think of—she walked back to the connecting door and put her ear against it. From the other side came the sound of water running.

"She's running a bath, I think," she muttered, and very carefully she slid the key back under the door to the other side. "Maybe if she sees it, she'll just think it fell out of the keyhole."

"But the door's unlocked now," Becca pointed out.

"Maybe she won't notice that," said Norah. But she didn't feel very hopeful.

"Our first day here, and I've already messed things up," moaned Becca.

She got no sympathy from her brother. "Serves you right for being so nosey," he declared.

Norah eased open the door from Andrew's room to the hall. "Come on, Becca," she urged. "The coast is clear. Let's get to our room while we can."

"Oh, right!" Andrew said sarcastically. "Now she'll think I was the one who snooped."

Back in their own room, in guilty silence, the girls divided their clothing between the four drawers in the huge bureau and got ready for bed. Becca was the first to slide her feet under the covers. "Ooh, it's freezing in here," she complained. "These sheets are like ice!"

"I always leave my socks on," Norah advised, tossing Becca's back up to her.

Suddenly, someone knocked on the door. "Don't answer it!" Becca begged and dove under the covers.

But it was Andrew who stuck his head inside. "Just me," he announced. "You haven't gone to bed yet, have you?"

"Not yet," said Norah. "I can't find where I put my hairbrush. And I forgot to tell you to open your door to the hall before you get into bed. The heat comes up from downstairs."

Andrew entered the room. "I noticed a bookcase in here before," he said, "and I've got nothing to read." He strolled around the big bed to have a look at the shelves on the other side.

"Those books are really ancient," Norah told him. "I've already checked." She unearthed her hairbrush from a pile of clothing she'd stuffed into the top drawer. "I've been so bored here that I've finished the two books I brought with me. I'll lend them to you if you'd like. They're right on top of the bookcase."

"No, they're not," Andrew told her. "I see what you mean about ancient, though." He was crawling along, reading book titles out loud. "Who is Horatio Alger Jr., anyway? Holy, d'you know when this book was published? 1884."

"I put my books right there, next to the lamp," said Norah, coming to join him. She crouched down beside her cousin to examine the shelves.

"Here they are!" she cried, drawing two paperbacks out from between some other books on the second shelf. "They must have fallen off the top, I guess, and Aunt Caroline put them in with the others." She offered them to Andrew. "I'm hoping Mom has a book for me for Christmas."

"Thanks, but those are not really what I like to read," Andrew replied, after glancing at the girl detective on the covers.

"You'd think Aunt Caroline should have known they were mine," Norah remarked, turning the paperbacks over in her hands. "My name is right inside the cover."

When she opened one of the books to show the others where she'd written "Norah B.", a sheaf of papers spilled out onto the bed.

"Hey, you bring your homework with you, Norah?" Andrew teased.

"This stuff's not mine." Norah gathered up the strange sheets of paper. "I wonder what it is." She sat down on the bed and riffled through the mysterious pages.

Curious, Becca knelt beside her. "What is it?" she asked.

Norah shook her head, reading slowly. "It's in handwriting, but it looks like a play or something. See, these are stage directions. Isn't that weird?"

"Would you mind if I took that to my room to read?" Andrew asked. "It looks kind of interesting. And anything's better than lying there staring at the ceiling."

"Sure, you can read it first," Norah agreed, handing him the papers. Besides, she had other things to worry about at the moment.

When Andrew had returned to his room, Norah spread the extra blanket over the big bed and got in under the covers where Becca lay shivering. Her cousin slid her hand over to take Norah's. "I'm sorry, Norah, if I got us into trouble with Aunt Caroline," she said in a small voice.

Norah sighed. "That's okay. I know you didn't mean to, and I went into the room with you, after all."

In the middle of the night, Norah heard the creak and groan of the heating ducts expanding. Aunt Caroline had turned on the furnace. Becca gave a little moan in her sleep and threw one leg out over the covers. Still wide awake, Norah lay with her arms folded behind her head, praying Aunt Caroline had not seen the key on the floor of her room.

Fourteen

The first thing Norah noticed when she opened her eyes the next morning was a change in the colour of the light coming into the bedroom. And there was a muffled stillness in the air.

Could it be, she wondered, sliding off the bed and moving through the pale light to the window. It was! All the grass and dead leaves, all the mud in the lane were covered with a thin layer of fresh snow.

As she stood there, taking in the scene below the window, the events of the night before came back to her, filling her with dread.

Stealthily, she dressed, trying not to disturb the sleeping Becca. She needed to be alone with her thoughts. If Aunt Caroline had seen the key on the floor of her room, had she discovered the connecting door had been opened? What could the children expect from her this morning, if she had?

The drawer of the bureau creaked loudly when Norah tried to ease it shut. Becca immediately sat up, rubbing her eyes and studying her surroundings.

The younger girl bounced to the end of the bed where

she could see outside. "I knew we'd have snow for Christmas!" she cried.

"The ground's already covered," Norah told her.

Becca joined her at the window, shivering as she wrapped her arms around herself. "Didn't I tell you if you came to Ontario we'd give you a white Christmas?"

Andrew poked his head in from the hall at that moment. "Actually, in Ontario," he informed them, coming into the room, "only one Christmas in three is white." He jabbed a finger into the back of his pajama-clad sister. "You not dressed yet, lazybones?"

Andrew carried the sheaf of papers he'd borrowed last evening. "I'm bringing these back, Norah," he said, waving them at her. "It's really cool. You should read it sometime."

"I think I'd feel like I was reading somebody's mail if I read this," Becca said, looking at the pages her brother laid on the bed. "It's all in somebody's handwriting."

"Well, it's not a letter," Andrew pointed out. "It's a little play. Hey, Norah, you don't suppose your aunt writes plays, do you?"

"I doubt it," said Norah. "But we could ask her. And she did take in boarders. Remember the guy who left the television? Maybe he was the one who wrote it."

"I'm going to ask her," Andrew decided. He gathered the pages again and set them on top of the bureau. "Hurry and get dressed, Becca," he said over his shoulder, as he left the room.

"Do you think Aunt Caroline figured out we were in her bedroom last night?" Becca worried. She'd laid out her jeans and a red, turtleneck sweater, but dawdled over taking off her pyjamas.

"I hope not," Norah admitted. For her part, she was content to sit on the bed and wait for her cousin, for as long as it took.

"Are you scared, Norah?" Becca asked, unbuttoning.

Norah winced. "Not scared, exactly. And the way I see it, we might as well get it over with. We have to face her sometime, you know."

When the little girl was finally ready, they descended the stairs to the dining room together. "I'm going to keep my fingers crossed," Becca whispered. "Just in case."

Once all three children were seated at the table, Aunt Caroline, wearing her usual grim expression, dished great gobs of cooked oatmeal into everyone's bowl. The children bent their heads over the food, scarcely looking up until the porridge was gone.

Andrew was the first to break the uncomfortable silence. "We found a play in the bookcase upstairs, Aunt Caroline," he said in a casual tone. "Any idea who could have written it?"

"Someone other than William Shakespeare, you mean?" Aunt Caroline looked at him over the top of her glasses.

"Oh, Aunt Caroline." Becca's voice trembled with relief. "You're so funny!"

"This play is handwritten," explained Andrew, ignoring his sister.

"I thought, maybe one of your boarders," Norah suggested as she returned the lid to the jar of brown sugar. "Were any of them writers?"

"My boarders?"

"You said you had a man boarding here."

"Once," Aunt Caroline conceded, crossly. "Against my better judgement. He was the brother of the man who delivers my groceries. I was doing him a favour, but I was never so glad to see anyone leave as I was him."

"Maybe you are a writer, Aunt Caroline," Becca piped up. "And we never knew it!"

"Hardly!" the woman replied, squashing the notion. "You're apt to find anything on those bookshelves. Some of those books have been in this house since my father's time."

"Then you don't mind if we read the play?" Norah asked.

"Not in the least," Aunt Caroline replied. "Do whatever it takes to keep yourselves occupied."

Andrew got up, folded his napkin and pushed his chair back under the table. "I don't know about you two, but I'm going outside to enjoy the snow," he announced, "before it all disappears."

"Me too," said Becca. "May we be excused, please?"

This display of good manners seemed to impress the old lady, and she bestowed a rare smile on Becca. Perhaps, thought Norah hopefully when she saw that smile, Aunt Caroline hadn't noticed the key she'd shoved back under the door.

That notion was quickly dashed, however, when the girls reached the top of the stairs after breakfast. For the first time since Norah's arrival, the door to Aunt Caroline's room stood open.

Norah tiptoed across the hall to take a peek. As she would have expected, her aunt's bed was already made up. The large key was back in the lock. But the photograph that had been tucked into the mirror was gone.

Fifteen

Andrew was plumping the pillows on the bed when the girls scurried into his room. Without a word, Norah crossed to the connecting door and tried the knob. It was locked.

"She knows!" she groaned. "Aunt Caroline not only picked up the key, but she locked the door again."

"She didn't say anything about it at breakfast, though," Becca pointed out. "Maybe she's not mad at us."

"Oh, she's mad at you all right." Her brother glowered at her. "She just hasn't decided what to do with you yet." Then he saw the stricken look on his little sister's face. "Just kidding," he admitted. "Anyway, what's done is done. Who knows, Norah, maybe your aunt has decided to forgive you for being a couple of snoops."

"I wonder what she did with the picture we were looking at," Norah puzzled. She took a seat on the only chair in the room.

Andrew asked, "What picture?"

"There was a black and white photo of some little kid sitting on a pony," Norah explained. "It was stuck up on her mirror yesterday. Now it's gone."

Andrew shrugged. "Maybe she was just tidying up and put it away."

Norah shook her head. "It had been there a long time; it had started to curl, even. Besides, it's funny that she'd take it down, just after we'd seen it."

"So, who was in the picture?"

"I don't know. Someone special, since it's the only picture I've seen in the whole house."

Andrew finished stuffing yesterday's clothing back into his pack and kicked it under the bed.

"I've been thinking," Norah said. "Now that there's snow on the ground, today might be a good day to see if Jody's still hanging around. We should be able to see his tracks this morning, if he's out there."

"Excellent idea," Andrew agreed.

"If we find him, I'll introduce you to him," Norah promised. She got up to leave.

Becca didn't think tracking the boy was something she wanted to do. "We don't know anything about him," she cautioned. "Maybe he's dangerous or something. You said you thought he was watching the house."

"But he's not dangerous at all, Becca," Norah told her.

"Well, maybe I'll just stay here and keep Aunt Caroline company anyway," was Becca's suggestion.

"Not a good idea," said Andrew. "Especially not after last night. Get your jacket and boots on and come with us. If Norah says this kid's okay, then I believe her."

Becca clumped unhappily down the stairs behind the other two. When the children pushed through the swinging door to the kitchen, they found Aunt Caroline fiercely beating something in an earthenware bowl. One look at the no-nonsense expression on the woman's face and Becca decided she would join the others after all.

As they stood surveying the snow-covered lawn from the back step, Andrew took command, warning the girls to move across the yard together, so as not to leave too many fresh tracks in the snow.

"The first time I saw Jody, he was just standing right about here," Norah said, indicating the opening in the hedge. "Next time, he was inside the yard. He told me later he was taking a shortcut to the village, passing by the house, he said. But if that was true, he'd hardly come all the way into the yard."

"I think we should follow the path then," Andrew decided. "See if we can spot his tracks."

"Really? I'd much rather stay here, Andrew." Becca scuffed at the snow with her boot. "I don't want to go into the woods. Why don't we try to build a snowman?"

"Snow's not packy enough for a snowman," her brother informed her. "And you'll be building it all by yourself, because Norah's coming to show us the way."

"But Norah got lost in the woods the last time," said Becca.

"It'll be okay, Becca," Norah promised. "Jody showed me the way to get around the pond. That's where I got mixed up. Anyway, the woods aren't dark, and the village isn't far."

"We're going all the way to the village?" The little girl's voice rose.

"This is a shortcut, Becca," Andrew pointed out. "Look. I've got some money in my pocket. Maybe we could find a place to buy some hot chocolate when we get there."

"Sure we can," Norah agreed. "There's a coffee shop in town. We could have a rest and get warmed up before we start back."

"Okay, Becca?" Andrew put a hand on his sister's shoulder, urging her forward.

"Hot chocolate with marshmallows," Becca grumbled, wriggling out of her brother's grasp. She stepped onto the path behind Norah.

After a few minutes of trudging single file through the trees, Norah turned to the little girl. "See? What did I tell you? It's nice in here, isn't it?" Snow sifted down through the bare branches and onto her upturned face, catching in her eyelashes.

"It's kind of like a church," Becca admitted. "You can't even hear the wind, the trees are so tall."

Andrew kept his eyes trained on the path. Except for the tracks of some small animals, there were no other footprints to be seen.

Norah stopped them at the place where she had seen Jody come out onto the path the first time and turn to go the other way.

"There aren't any trails going off this one in any other direction," objected Andrew. "See, the brush is really thick here."

"I know, but when I looked up I saw him come through, right about here," Norah insisted. "I yelled at him, but he didn't hear me. He just walked on down the path towards town."

"I think you must be wrong about that," Andrew

muttered, and he moved away again. The girls followed his determined back.

When they arrived at the place with all the gnawed tree stumps, Norah steered them to the left, skirting the beaver pond and picking up the trail again on the other side.

It had been snowing steadily since daylight, and by the time the three reached the far side of the woods, they discovered that the wind had picked up and was blowing snow directly into their faces. And still no sign of the boy.

They came out of the trees and started across the open field, where the full force of the wind met them, head on. Now there was no real path to follow, and Norah stopped to try to get her bearings. "There's a fence somewhere we have to follow," she remembered, peering out through the driving snow. "We have to keep going west, anyway. We'll come out at the edge of town."

"Which way is west?" Andrew inquired. He was walking backwards now to keep the wind behind him.

Becca was shivering. "Here, let me put your scarf around your collar," Norah offered.

Holding her own mittens between her knees, she raised the little girl's collar up around her ears, pulling her toque lower and knotting the scarf under her reddened chin.

"How much farther?" Becca asked, through chattering teeth.

Norah squinted into the snow. She had thought from here that she should be able to see the sheds of the lumberyard that marked the eastern limits of the town. "Not too much farther," she guessed.

"Oh, Norah," wailed Becca, "I just knew we'd get lost! Remember? I didn't want to come in the first place."

Sixteen

"We are not lost, Becca," Andrew declared. "Look. You can still see the woods behind us. As long as we keep them at our backs, we're okay."

But when Norah swung around in the same direction, she was alarmed to see that where the forest should have been, there was only a darker blur on the all-white landscape. "I think we'd better turn back, Andrew," she admitted. "Becca is freezing, and I'm starting to lose the feeling in my feet."

Andrew hesitated, stamping his own feet and slapping mittened hands against his sides. But another look at his little sister's eyes, tearing in the wind, persuaded him. "Okay. We'll go back, I guess. We'd never be able to track anyone in this heavy snow anyway."

"Right," Norah agreed. "Besides, wherever Jody's staying, he's not out in this."

With the stinging snow at their backs, they hurried for the shelter of the trees again. The snow had already covered their original tracks, and Norah stopped a moment, uncertain of where they had exited the woods.

Doggedly, Andrew plunged ahead. "Here's the path!"

he called, the wind whipping the words from his mouth.

"Are you positive this is the right way?" Norah gasped, after they had followed him for a few minutes. It looked very different to her. She was sure the path they had taken had not been as overgrown as this one. She was having to hold branches aside so that they didn't snap back at Becca, stumbling along behind.

It was a relief to be out of the wind, though. "I'm sure we can find a hot drink in Aunt Caroline's kitchen," Norah encouraged, twisting a sapling out of Becca's way. When Becca said nothing, Norah bent to look into her face. The little girl managed a smile through lips stiff with cold. "But I bet she hasn't got any marshmallows," she said in a thin voice.

Andrew was in front, turning to walk backwards every now and then to check the girls' progress. "It can't be much farther," he told them. "Maybe you guys would like to read that play when we get back."

"Andrew, stop a minute," Norah insisted. "I don't think this is the way we came. In fact, I'm sure it isn't."

Becca started to whimper, and her brother backtracked to her side. "Come on, Becca," he urged. "If you were still little, I'd carry you on my back. Remember we used to do that?" He put a protective arm around her, moving her forward.

Norah had pushed ahead of them. "Hey, come here, you guys!" she cried suddenly. "I found something. Look at this!"

She parted the bushes for the others, and to everyone's surprise, they found themselves facing a small shed, almost buried in the undergrowth. "It's an old cabin or something!"

"I bet it's a sugar shack," Andrew said. "But whatever, we can stop here and rest a bit."

"I don't want to go into that place, Andrew." Becca's voice trembled.

"You don't have to. Stay here, and I'll go check it out, make sure there're no animals inside."

The door of the shed was partially open, and a thin wedge of snow had worked its way across the dirt floor. "It's empty," declared Andrew as he shoved the door wider and went in. Norah was right behind him. She could feel Becca's hand against her back.

There was one window in the shed with four cracked panes of glass, and a round hole in the roof where once a stovepipe had been. A workbench or counter was attached to the far wall, and part of a straw broom lay on a floor littered in dead leaves and animal droppings. Andrew crouched down to inspect them.

"What kind of animal, do you think?" Norah asked.

"Porcupine, most likely," he replied. "See how it has chewed the handle off the broom? There would have been salt on it from someone's hands, and that's what the porcupines go for." He looked up at his sister, who was peering at him from behind Norah. "There's nothing in here, Becca. And there's so much brush and stuff covering the roof that it's still pretty dry inside. Do you think we should wait here till the snow lets up?"

"But there's nothing to sit on," Becca complained. "And what if whoever owns this place comes back and finds us here?"

"There hasn't been anyone in here in years," her

brother assured her. "Unless you count the porcupines."

But Norah too was having second thoughts about stopping there. "I don't really think it's a good idea anyway, Andrew," she said. "We've got to keep going. Aunt Caroline will be worrying about us."

She took hold of Becca's hand. "Come on, Bec. We can't be that far from home. It's been at least twenty minutes since we started back." She didn't tell her young cousin that there was a good chance that for the best part of that twenty minutes, they had been on the wrong trail.

Reluctantly, Andrew pulled the door of the shed closed as far as it would go and followed the girls out into the snow again. He found Norah investigating the brush behind the shed. "Not that way, Norah. We've got to go back out the way we came in," he told her. "Retrace our steps."

Norah shook her head. "I don't think so. What you thought was the trail, Andrew, ended up at this place. There's got to be a way out of here." Suddenly, she disappeared.

Seconds later, they heard her from the other side. "Through here!" Norah cried. "It's this way! You can get through here, and I'm standing on the other path!"

Andrew, with Becca in tow, immediately broke through the brush to join her. "Wow," he marvelled, looking back at where they'd come out. "Who would have thought you could get through there? You were right, Norah. This is the path we came down."

"Okay, Becca." Norah grabbed the little girl's mittened hand again. "Let's jog!"

A short time later, Andrew, who had taken the lead again, called back to them triumphantly, "Look, Becca, I can see the house from here! We're almost home!"

Sure enough, the dark outline of the Stoppard house appeared ahead of them, out of the snow. They all ran the last few metres, bursting through the opening in the cedars and plunging across the backyard to the door. The heat of the kitchen rushed out to enfold them.

Seventeen

When the three cousins burst through the back door and into the house, they discovered the kitchen counter was lined with plastic grocery bags. Aunt Caroline was nowhere in sight. They hung their snowy jackets behind the stove and draped their mitts over the towel rack to dry.

As Becca sat on the floor, holding her stockinged toes in her hands and rocking to and fro, Aunt Caroline bustled into the room. "Where on earth have you been?" she fumed. "I was getting worried about you."

"We were going to walk to the village, but we turned back when the snow got so heavy," Norah explained. "We're sorry to have worried you."

"It's a good thing that you did turn back," declared Aunt Caroline. "The man with the groceries said the roads were getting bad. He was lucky to get out of the lane." She stepped around Becca on the floor. "If there's one more thing I don't need, it's having him stranded here."

"We found an old shed in the woods just now, Aunt Caroline," Norah told her. "It's well-hidden, but not too far from here really. Do you know what it could have been used for?"

"The bushes have grown up all around it," Andrew added. "But there was a place where there used to be a stove pipe through the roof, and with all the maple trees, I thought maybe it used to be a sugar shack."

"I have no idea what it was," Aunt Caroline retorted. "But I would have thought you would know better than to go poking around in places where you don't belong."

In the silence that followed that remark, Becca and Norah exchanged guilty looks. Was she referring to last evening, Norah wondered?

"Now, run along out of here," Aunt Caroline said finally, "and let me get these things put away. I've lit the fire in the den for you."

"Norah?" Becca croaked in a hoarse whisper, "what about the hot chocolate?"

"Hot chocolate?" Aunt Caroline swung around. "I don't keep such a thing in the house." Becca's face fell. "I can make cocoa though, if that would suit you."

"That would be perfect," Norah said. "And we can make it ourselves, actually."

Aunt Caroline bristled. "Do you think I want three extra bodies in my kitchen when I have work to do? Off with you now. Rebecca will stay and make the cocoa."

"Wow," muttered Andrew as he and Norah crossed the hall. "What did Becca do to get on her good side all of a sudden?"

"She's just Becca, I guess," Norah said, with a shrug.

"She's pretty good at the poor-little-me act, you mean," her cousin remarked.

The fire in the den was inviting, and the two plopped

down in the leather armchairs. They held out hands and feet towards the flame, grateful for the warmth.

After a few minutes Andrew asked, "When we discovered the old shed in the woods just now, didn't you think we had found the place where that boy Jody was hiding out?"

"No way," declared Norah. "You said yourself no one had been there in years."

"It was the first thing I thought of," Andrew admitted, sounding disappointed. "Until I saw the inside of it." He was picking at the threads around a tear in the knee of his jeans. "I guess it's a good thing you didn't listen to me, Norah, but found the trail back yourself. We might still be walking."

"I'll tell you one good thing about the route you took, though," Norah pointed out. "It was so far past the place where we'd left the woods, that we missed the beaver pond altogether."

She got out of her chair. "I'm going up to get that play we found last night," she announced. "I want to read it. Will you still be here when I get back?"

"Are you kidding?" Andrew asked, yawning widely. "I'm so comfortable here, I might never move." He had closed his eyes by the time Norah returned.

For the next twenty minutes Norah sat, legs curled under her, absorbing the heat from the fire and reading the handwritten play. Andrew drowsed nearby. Becca delivered two mugs of hot cocoa to them with a smug smile and promptly disappeared again.

When Norah laid down the last sheet of paper,

93

Andrew opened his eyes. "So, what do you think?" he asked.

"It's okay. Kind of weird, though. I mean, when the man asks the boy who he is, and the boy tells the man that he is him, when he was fifteen."

Andrew nodded. "It was the boy that got my interest. How no one could see him except the young man. It kind of makes me think about that boy you've been seeing."

"What are you saying?" Norah frowned. "That no one can see Jody except me? That he's invisible?"

"Well, has your aunt or anyone else said they saw him?"

"There is no one else, Andrew. Sure Aunt Caroline denied he was there when he was. But he's real! I talked to him. I can tell you what he said, what he was wearing, how his teeth were a little crooked." Norah put a finger on her two front teeth. "See these two here? His were sort of crossed, kind of like mine are. I sure wasn't imagining him."

"Okay, okay." Andrew held up his hands in a gesture of surrender. "Forget it. Just hear me out on my next theory, will you? I say that whoever wrote this play lived right here in this house."

"Why? Because of the gift of the birdfeeder at the end? Lots of people have birdfeeders. Well, maybe not as many as Aunt Caroline."

"Not just because of the birdfeeder," Andrew insisted. "But do you really think someone writing a play would just drop it off here?"

"Oh, I see what you mean," Norah said. "I guess not. The person who wrote it must have been staying in this house. Otherwise, why would it be here, in its handwritten form?"

"My theory, exactly," said Andrew with satisfaction.

Norah thumbed back through the pages. "I wonder what Aunt Caroline would make of this."

"Think she'd read it?" Andrew asked.

"Probably wouldn't have time," said Norah. "But after we've all gone home, she might."

"Hey, I've got a cool idea!" Andrew slapped the leather arms of his chair and jumped to his feet. "Your aunt wouldn't *have* to read it, if we put it on for her at Christmas!"

Norah scowled up at him. "Who do you mean by we? You and me and Becca?"

"Sure, why not? We're supposed to have an old-fashioned Christmas here this year. In the old days, people made their own entertainment, didn't they? We could practise it and put it on for the grownups when they get here."

Norah considered the idea. "It would give us something to do, I guess. But the others will be here day after tomorrow, you know."

"Yeah, but the play's not too long, and there are only two characters in it. Well, there's the nurse, but she has no lines. That would be the perfect part for Becca!"

"It might be kind of fun." Slowly, Norah uncurled herself from the chair. "But we should run the idea by Aunt Caroline first. And where is Becca, anyway?"

As they walked out into the hall together, Andrew sniffed the air. "My mouth is watering," he said. "Something sure smells good."

The house was full of the enticing aroma of cinnamon and ginger. "If you didn't know better," Norah said, "you'd think it was starting to smell like Christmas around here."

They followed their noses to the kitchen. From the other side of the door came the low sound of voices in companionable conversation. Norah paused before pushing the door open, giving Andrew a puzzled look. "What's going on in here, I wonder?" she muttered.

Eighteen

Wrapped in one of Aunt Caroline's crisp aprons, Becca perched on a stool in the kitchen, lifting cookies off a baking sheet and onto a cooling rack. Aunt Caroline was wrestling a huge turkey into the bottom of the fridge.

"Have you ever seen anyone hanging around your property, Aunt Caroline?" Becca asked. She looked up when the other two entered the room and waved her spatula at them.

"Certainly not," vowed Aunt Caroline. She slammed the fridge door. "Have you?"

"No, but Norah has," Becca bragged.

"I told you, Aunt Caroline," Norah said, fighting the urge to snatch a warm cookie off the tray. "He was just a kid."

"Well, if anyone's hanging around here, kid or not, I'll call the police. They'll send him packing."

"Becca," Andrew chided, a worried eye on Aunt Caroline, "are you supposed to be in here?"

"Sure," the little girl replied. "I'm helping."

"But we weren't going to bother Great-aunt Caroline. Remember?" her brother said, through clenched teeth.

"Leave her be," ordered Caroline Stoppard. "And one cookie, Norah. You may have one cookie. Eating between meals is a habit to be avoided at all costs."

It came as no surprise to Norah, when they asked about practising the play and putting it on as a Christmas entertainment, that Aunt Caroline was only interested in having them stay out from underfoot.

"We'll practise it upstairs, in one of our rooms," Andrew promised. "It'll keep us busy till the others get here."

Becca was less than eager to participate. "I don't really want to be in a play, Andrew," she pouted.

"Come on, Becca. Don't spoil it. There's even one part that has no lines."

"Go along now, Rebecca," Aunt Caroline said, shooing them all towards the kitchen door. "You've done all you can, and I'm already late getting lunch on."

It wasn't until after they had finished the noon meal that Norah and Andrew were able to persuade Becca to sit still long enough for them to read the play aloud to her. "Why don't you just tell me what it's about?" the little girl suggested, slumping into the den behind them.

"It's called 'The Gift,'" Norah began, "and it's about a mysterious boy who visits a lonely, young man."

"What's mysterious about him?" Becca interrupted.

"The only person who can see him is the young man," Norah explained. "Anyway, the young man is in a convalescent hospital when the boy visits him." She anticipated Becca's next question. "That's a hospital where people who are getting over being sick, but who are still not ready to go back to their normal lives, go to finish getting better."

Becca dropped into one of the armchairs and yawned. "So, what was the matter with the young man? Why was he in the hospital?"

"He was recovering from tuberculosis, TB for short. That's a lung disease. He'd been in another hospital, a TB sanitarium, but before he was well enough to go back home to university, he had to regain his strength."

Andrew slid forward in his chair and eagerly took up the story. "So the two become friends. The young man— the invalid—likes to draw, and he sketches this boy that he sees sitting on a stone wall at the edge of the hospital property. At first, he doesn't even think the boy is real. He thinks he might be a garden statue; the boy sits that still.

"But when his nurse goes back inside and leaves them alone, the young man sees the boy shift position. The next thing you know, they start up a conversation, and after a while the boy comes over to him and asks what he is drawing."

"And the boy keeps coming back." Norah jumped in again. "Every day, he comes to see how the drawing is coming along. On the day that the young man is leaving the hospital, he gives the finished picture to the boy as a present. In return, the boy brings the young man something that he has made himself." She sat back, waiting for Becca's question, leaving the best part for last.

Instead, Becca wrinkled her nose. "Is that all there is to it?"

"We told you it isn't a very long play," said Andrew. "That's why we think we can learn it in the two days we have left before the others get here."

"Don't the characters even have names?" Becca grumbled. "You keep saying the young man and the boy."

"They have names," Norah told her. "But in the stage notes they are just called the young man and the boy. It comes out in the play that the boy's name is Jamie, and the man's name is James."

"Sounds to me like they have the same name," muttered Becca. Norah and Andrew exchanged knowing glances.

"And you know what else is strange?" Norah continued. "The present the boy brings to the young man, the gift he has made himself. Guess what it is."

"What?"

"A birdfeeder."

"A birdfeeder?" Becca's eyes suddenly grew very large. "That's funny. But he's just an imaginary boy, isn't he?"

"I'm not sure." Andrew thumbed back through the pages. "I don't think the young man was sure either. Here, let me read that part to you. Okay, here it is.

"The young man is out on the patio behind the hospital. The boy has come down from the stone wall and come around behind the man's wheelchair, to look at what he is sketching.

"Boy: Is that how I look to you?

Young man: I thought I'd captured you very well.

(Boy considers the sketch, his head to one side)

Young man: I get the impression you don't think much of my work.

Boy: Oh, I think you are a good artist, all right. I'm

just interested in seeing how you draw me.

Young man: Why is that?

Boy: Because I am you.

Young man: I beg your pardon?

Boy: You know how you said that your nurse couldn't see me? It's true; she can't. Nor can anyone else but you.

Young man: You're in my imagination, then.

Boy: Not exactly. I am you, as you were at age fifteen. My name is Jamie. I'm surprised you didn't recognize me.

Young man: That's funny, you know. My mother used to call me Jamie. I remember the time I told her I wished she wouldn't, that I was too grown up for such names.

Boy: And now? What do people call you now?

Young man: James. It is my name, after all. Look, I told you why I have to be here. Why are you here?

Boy: To keep you company.

Young man: You were here before, weren't you? That first day, early in the morning. I saw footprints across the grass, in the frost. Someone had come onto the property from the path through the trees.

Boy: I was waiting for you.

Young man (shaking his head): This doesn't make any sense. I must still be sick. You can't be me when I am me. We can't both be in the same place at once.

Boy: Why fight it? Just accept it. I want to be your friend. You said you'd been feeling lonely."

Andrew stopped reading and looked up at his sister, who had gone to the window to look out at the falling snow.

"I don't get it," Becca said, turning away from the window with a frown. She heaved a sigh of resignation. "Oh, all right. If I say I'll be in it, can I have a nurse's uniform?"

"Sure," Norah agreed. "I bet we can find a white blouse around here, and I know Aunt Caroline has some white aprons."

"And one of those little caps nurses used to wear?"

"Right," Andrew promised. "We can probably make a nurse's cap, can't we, Norah? So, will you be in it, Becca?"

"I guess," his sister said. She perched herself on the arm of Norah's chair.

"All right!" Andrew exclaimed. "Now, we'll need to borrow one of Aunt Caroline's birdfeeders for the play. Do you think she'd lend us one?"

"I'll ask her," Becca offered, brightening. "She'll let us borrow one if I ask her."

"On second thought, I can make that too," her brother said. "You just ask her for something to wear for a nurse's uniform."

"Whatever," Becca agreed. "I'm not afraid of Aunt Caroline. Not any more."

Andrew glared at her. "Neither am I. And unlike you, I have no reason to be afraid of her."

"Oh, that," said Becca, rolling her eyes. "I told her we'd been in her room that time."

Norah gulped. "You did what?"

"I told her I was the one who opened her bedroom door to look inside, that I just wondered what it would be like."

"I can't believe you had the nerve, Becca," Norah said.

"Well, I did. I said you were with me, but that it was my idea and that when we heard her coming, we ducked into Andrew's room."

"What did she say to that?" asked Norah.

Becca shrugged. "Not much. Actually, she didn't say anything at all for a while, just looked at me, like she was thinking. I got a little scared then. But all she said was something about children being curious creatures, that she guessed that's how we learn about things."

"And she wasn't mad?"

"Nope," Becca replied. "So, I'll ask her if we can borrow one of her birdfeeders, if you like."

"Never mind!" decided Andrew. "Anyway, those feeders outside are full of seed. I can make one out of cardboard. It doesn't have to be weatherproof, for the play. We can use the box the snow globe came in.

"And I was thinking," he continued. "We could use the dining room as the stage. We can push the big table against the wall, and the audience can sit in the living room, on the other side of the arch."

"Too bad we don't have a curtain," Norah realized. "Even though the scenery is the same, the second act takes place weeks later, after James and Jamie have had time to get to know each other."

"We don't need a curtain," insisted Andrew. "We'll just turn out the lights between acts."

"Do we have enough people, though?" Becca wondered. "There must be other patients, if it's a hospital. Where are we going to get more people?"

Norah said, "We don't need more people. There's no mention of anyone else. Just the nurse who comes and goes. She wheels the sick, young man outside, fetches things for him. In the second act, the man is able to walk around the grounds by himself. The nurse isn't even in it."

Andrew got to his feet and stretched himself to his full height. "Since I am the tallest," he said, "I'll play the young man. Okay? You, Norah, can be the mysterious boy."

Becca looked thoughtful. "The boy in the play reminds me of the boy you told us about, Norah."

"That's the same thing I thought when I read it," her brother agreed.

"So," Becca went on, "do you think the boy in the play is real, or just in the imagination of the young man?"

"That's the question, I guess," Norah admitted. "We don't know. But I do know that the boy I keep seeing is real enough. I talked to him, and his name is Jody."

"But you haven't seen him since we got here, have you?" asked Andrew.

"I thought I did once. When we were all in the garden. But maybe it was just a bird or something."

"So you haven't actually seen him since we arrived."

"No, but I haven't been looking either. Except today with you guys, for his footprints."

"Were you looking for him before?" Becca was curious. She swivelled around on the arm of the chair to face her cousin.

"Maybe I was," Norah realized. "I was pretty lonely before you guys got here."

"So was the young man, in the play," said Andrew. "Did you ever stop to think that maybe Jody was looking for you?"

"No," Norah said, wrinkling her brow. "Why would he?"

*   *   *

All night the snow fell, piling up around the shed in the trees, muffling any sound. Inside, under the light of the coal oil lantern, Jody was putting the finishing touches on his creation.

He stood back to admire his work. He was much more skilled at carpentry now, he realized with satisfaction. This birdfeeder was a far cry from his first effort. How long ago was that? Must be over forty years.

Soon, Jody knew, he would have no further need of this hiding place. It wouldn't be long now. And after he was gone, the little shed would be returned to the forest around it.

Nineteen

When the red van with the Christmas tree tied on top pulled up in front of the Stoppard house shortly after noon on Christmas Eve, Becca launched herself off the step and into the arms of her startled parents.

"Such an exuberant child," remarked Aunt Caroline, watching from the doorway. She stepped back inside to await formal introductions to this latest horde of visitors.

The three children were immediately enlisted to help unload the van, making numerous trips back and forth, arms loaded with bags and boxes, and tracking in snow.

"I hope you were ready for the invasion," Uncle Richard teased, in his loud, cheery voice. He didn't give Aunt Caroline time to respond before he set a long package in her hands. "Smoked salmon," he said, with a wink. "A real treat. You'll love it."

The front hall quickly filled with people shedding winter coats and boots, pieces of luggage, boxes of ornaments and yards of garland. Once released from its sheath of mesh, the Christmas tree opened out to such an amazing size that the only place for it was right there in the entrance hall, to the left of the curved staircase.

"It'll be perfect there," cried Ginny, hugging Norah for the tenth time. "And we don't have to move any furniture to fit it in. Oh and snow, darling! Isn't it wonderful?"

Becca hopped from one stair to the next, waiting for her father to level the tree stand. "*We* have a special surprise for everyone tonight," she boasted. "We are going to put on a play."

"No kidding?" Uncle Richard sat back on his heels and peered up at her. "When did you three come up with a play?"

"It was a script that we found in our bedroom here. It had just enough parts that we could do it."

"Imagine you kids spending your holiday practising a play," Auntie Gwen purred. She was lining up all the overshoes inside the front door. "Aren't they the most amazing youngsters?"

Aunt Caroline watched the proceedings down the length of her nose. "I must warn you that I have no idea what this play is about," she said. "So please don't hold me responsible. All I asked was that the children stay out from underfoot."

"And did they?" Uncle Richard inquired, eyes twinkling.

"They did, indeed," conceded Aunt Caroline.

"Marvellous! You'll have to let us in on your secret."

The house didn't seem nearly as big now, with the addition of three adults and an oversized Christmas tree.

"Oh, my!" Auntie Gwen complained, as the two younger women prepared to take over the kitchen. "Caroline, your fridge is already full." She backed away, arms loaded with turnips and sweet potatoes and bags of salad greens.

"Before the stores close," Ginny promised, "Gwen and I will go into town to pick up whatever you think we have forgotten."

"By the looks of it, I doubt you've forgotten anything," Aunt Caroline observed sourly.

"We'll just leave the pies and the juice in the coolers," Ginny decided. "Here, Norah. Let's set them out on the back step. It's cold enough out there that they won't spoil."

Ginny stepped out the back door. "My goodness!" she exclaimed. "Will you look at that!"

Norah had picked up one of the coolers. She kept her back against the door to hold it open. "Look at what?" she asked.

"The collection of birdfeeders! I've never seen so many!" Lifting the smaller cooler out of Norah's hands, Ginny set it beside the first one on the step. "And here's a feeder she had no place to hang, I guess."

Puzzled, Norah came out onto the step herself. "I've never seen that birdfeeder before," she said.

Ginny picked it up and examined it more closely. "All it needs is a wire to hang it by. Maybe Richard could attach some to the sides here. Oh look, Norah! It has your name on it."

"It can't have!"

"See for yourself, then. 'Merry Christmas, Norah,'" Ginny read. "It's a present from someone. For you, dear."

"It can't be!" Norah sputtered. She read the inscription burned into the bottom of the feeder. "But I don't know anyone here," she said, wrinkling her brow. "Who would give me a present?"

"Maybe your Aunt Caroline?" Ginny suggested. "Come on. It's cold out here. Let's take it inside and find out."

"Whatcha got there?" Uncle Richard asked as the two re-entered the kitchen.

"I'm going to show you," said Ginny. She went through to the dining room and set the birdfeeder on the table there. "Look at this, everyone. I thought it was one of Caroline's collection, but it's got Norah's name on it." She smiled at Caroline Stoppard. "I hope I'm not spoiling someone's surprise."

The others gathered around to have a look. The birdfeeder was made of strips of bark, designed to look like a miniature log cabin, with a feeding porch on all four sides. The roof, which extended to the edge of the porch to provide shelter from the snow and rain, was hinged so that it lifted up to receive the birdseed.

"It's beautiful," proclaimed Auntie Gwen. "Look at those dear little cedar shakes on the roof, and I just love the tiny rail fence around the edge. It's just adorable!"

"Very well made," agreed Uncle Richard. "It would fetch a good dollar in a craft shop, I'm sure."

Everyone turned questioning eyes on Aunt Caroline. "How very strange," the woman said, growing suddenly pale. "Does Norah know where it came from?"

"Honestly, I have no idea," Norah protested. "Unless one of you is playing tricks on me."

"Oh, this is too weird," muttered Andrew. "A present! A birdfeeder!"

There were only two other people in the room who knew what he meant, and Becca was busy emptying a box of Christmas presents for the tree.

"Well, I'm sure the mystery will eventually solve itself," said Ginny. "Will you help me take my suitcase upstairs, Norah? Out of everyone's way? I've brought a couple of gifts with me that still need to be wrapped too."

*   *   *

Upstairs, Norah's mother opened her suitcase on the big bed in the room they would share. "So, you made a friend here after all," she said.

Norah gave her a blank look.

"The person who gave you the birdfeeder, I mean."

"I'm not really sure where it came from, Mom," Norah said, slowly. But an idea was starting to take shape in her mind. Could Jody have left it for her? She barely knew him, but she could think of no one else.

Ginny slid a silk blouse onto a hanger and hung it in the closet. "Well, I'm glad you were able to enjoy yourself, once your cousins got here anyway."

"We've had a good time," Norah agreed. "Having Becca and Andrew here was a whole lot better than being alone with Aunt Caroline."

"Why don't you tell me about your Great-aunt Caroline?" Ginny suggested, sitting on the bed and lowering the empty suitcase to the floor. "This is the first time I've met her too, you know. What do you think of her?"

Norah had no trouble answering that question. "She's

like nobody I've ever met. She's so strict, and bossy too. But I guess you've already found that out. Anything that might be fun, she thinks is a waste of time. Even watching television.

"And look at this house, how ugly it is!" Norah was gathering steam now. "I mean, there's nothing colourful or pretty here. She's got all kinds of art—oil paintings, even—in the spare room. They must have hung on the walls here once. But she's taken them all down!"

"Poor dear," Ginny remarked. "I wonder what would make her do that?"

Norah twisted a length of Christmas ribbon around and around her hand as she spoke. "It's like she doesn't allow herself any joy or anything, Mom. Except for her birds."

Ginny nodded. "It's obvious how much she cares for them." She looked into Norah's face and smiled. "Now, tell me the truth about that birdfeeder," she said.

Just at that moment, Becca came pounding up the stairs and knocked on the door. "Come on, you two!" she cried. "Aunt Caroline found an extension cord so we could plug in the lights. You've never seen such a beautiful tree!"

Uncle Richard made them all wait on the landing until he'd turned out the overhead light and switched on the tree's twinkling bulbs, for the full effect. It was dazzling. It seemed to Norah that Christmas was just what the Stoppard house needed—the sound of happy voices and the coloured lights pushing back the dark.

The grown-ups had brought everything for the evening meal, remembering even the chocolate sprinkles to top off dessert. Norah was sure Aunt Caroline had never been part of such a noisy feast. No one could resist Uncle Richard's infectious enthusiasm, although Norah noticed her great-aunt wince a little at his loud voice.

As soon as the supper dishes were cleared away, Andrew and his father moved the dining table to the far side of the room, and the girls arranged the chairs in the living room, ready for the entertainment. Aunt Caroline watched the operation from the kitchen door, frowning steadily. "Be very careful moving that table," she warned. "I don't want the legs loosened up."

"Come, dear, and sit down," Ginny invited, leading her to a small loveseat where they could sit together. "We'll have the best seat in the house."

Once the audience was settled, Andrew stood and faced them, clearing his throat ceremoniously. "Ladies and gentleman," he announced. "Our entertainment tonight is a play called 'The Gift.' The members of the cast are: Andrew Moore as James, the young man; Norah Bingham as Jamie, the boy; and Becca Moore as the nurse. The author of the play is, well, we don't know who she was."

"Unanimous," Becca prompted from the kitchen door that doubled as the wings.

"I think," Uncle Richard interjected with a chuckle, "the word is anonymous."

*　　*　　*

After the children had turned out the lights between acts and slipped into the kitchen to get ready for the final

112

scene, Norah turned to her cousins with a questioning look. "Do you think Aunt Caroline is okay?"

"Why?"

"She looks awfully white to me, has ever since this afternoon."

"It's probably just the excitement of having everyone here." Andrew was switching the dressing gown he'd borrowed for a sweater, now that his character, James, was well enough to stroll around the hospital grounds.

"I noticed it too," Becca whispered as she took off her apron, her part in the play over. "Just about the time the young man asks the nurse about the boy that he sees on the stone wall, Aunt Caroline made a funny sound. You know your line, Andrew: 'He didn't speak to me, but I have the feeling that he wants to tell me something.' That's when I heard it."

"It was likely Dad's stomach making noises," suggested Andrew, casually. "Did you see how much food he piled on his plate at supper? Okay. Ready, Norah? Becca, you go first. Scoot into the living room and find a seat."

Whenever she had the opportunity during the last act, Norah stole a look at her great-aunt. It was at the end of the play, when the boy brought his special present to the young man, that Aunt Caroline suddenly slapped a hand over her mouth.

"Are you okay, Auntie?" Norah heard Ginny inquire.

Aunt Caroline, eyes wide above the hand that covered her mouth, nodded, and the play came to an end.

Twenty

Becca stood with Norah and Andrew in the archway as they took their bows, following the presentation of the play. "That was wonderful," Ginny exclaimed when she finally stopped clapping.

Auntie Gwen was all smiles. "And what a lovely story, too," she remarked.

"Fantastic!" boomed Uncle Richard and got to his feet. "Now, can I get anyone an eggnog?"

Only Aunt Caroline remained silent.

"We'll put the table back for you now," Norah offered, wondering if this might have upset her great-aunt more than she had realized. She signalled to Andrew to help her.

"No, that's all right." Aunt Caroline waved away the offer with a weary gesture. "The table's fine till morning. Please just leave it." She pressed the tips of her fingers to her temples for a moment and closed her eyes.

"Is there something wrong?" Norah asked, crouching in front of the old lady. It was as if all the starch had gone out of Caroline Stoppard.

Ginny had her arm around the woman's shoulders. "I'm sure she's just tired, dear," she said to Norah.

"I am not tired." Aunt Caroline came to attention sharply. "I have scarcely been allowed to lift a finger around here all day."

"The beef then, at supper," suggested Auntie Gwen.

"No. Please. My digestion is fine. But I must ask the children something."

"Sure," said Andrew, coming to join them. "What is it?"

"Is that all there was to the play?"

"Yes," said Norah, surprised. "It was pretty short. Why?"

"I thought you might have left something out. Something the boy told the young man. Remember the man told his nurse he felt there was something the boy wanted to say to him?"

Andrew nodded slowly. "Yes, but we did the whole play, all that was written. You did like it, didn't you?"

Managing a weak smile, Aunt Caroline said, "You are all budding actors, to be sure. It's just that the play was a bit of a shock to me." She sat back in her seat and looked around at all the faces turned in her direction.

"How so?" asked Uncle Richard.

After taking a breath deep enough for all of them to hear, Caroline Stoppard continued, "It seems to have been based on something that really happened."

"It was? Then, do you know who wrote it?" asked Andrew.

"I do," declared Aunt Caroline, and suddenly she began to shake, unable to continue speaking for the chattering of her teeth.

"Would you like to lie down, dear?" Ginny offered.

She got quickly to her feet to allow room for the old lady to stretch out.

Aunt Caroline shook her head. She put one of her trembling hands over Norah's where it lay beside her on the loveseat. "It's…nerves," she assured them. "I get… like this whenever I have an attack of nerves. Just hang on a minute." She bit her bottom lip and wrapped her arms across her chest, as if trying to get a grip on herself before speaking again. "Your father wrote that play, Norah," she said finally. "Your husband, Ginny."

Ginny was nodding and smiling smugly, looking as if she had known all along. Norah was speechless. Everyone else waited.

"I had a feeling this was going to happen," Aunt Caroline said. "Ever since Norah said she saw that boy. And then this afternoon, the birdfeeder…"

"What do you mean?" Norah croaked.

"Years ago," Aunt Caroline went on, in a tremulous voice, "when he was a young man, twenty-one perhaps and still in university, your father came here where it was warm and dry to complete his recovery. He'd had tuberculosis. All I could do for him, really, was make sure he took his medication and got his rest."

She scanned the faces around her. "Joseph—he gave himself the name of James in the play, which he must have written since no one else knew the story—was my son."

"My father's name was Joseph," Norah interjected. "But he was your nephew."

Aunt Caroline shook her head again. "No, he was my son. And until now, I've never told a soul."

Norah scrambled to her feet. "Wait a minute! You're saying my *father* wrote this play? So it was my *father* who was visited by the boy who said he was him at age fifteen?"

"Cool," said Andrew.

"That's what I'm saying," Aunt Caroline agreed. "And now I have to wonder if the boy told him about our true relationship. That the woman, whom he thought was his aunt, was really his mother. Joseph never confronted me with the fact. But the boy might have told him. Although you say it was not in the script."

"It wasn't!" the children chorused.

Aunt Caroline stroked the network of blue veins on the back of her hands as she spoke, her voice filled with regret. "I had the opportunity to tell him myself while he was here, but I kept the promise I'd made to my sister at his birth. As it turned out, it was the one and only time I got to spend with my son."

"But how could he be your son?" Becca asked. "I thought Norah's father was your nephew."

"That's what everyone was supposed to think," admitted Aunt Caroline, settling her gaze on the little girl. "It's a long, sad story, Rebecca. But now I think it really must be told."

With that, Becca went to sit in Auntie Gwen's lap, where she wouldn't miss a word.

Caroline Stoppard took another deep breath. The worst of the trembling was over.

"Years ago, I met a man who came out here looking for work. He wasn't from these parts, but he'd joined a crew out of Hanley that was putting a new roof on my house.

After the job was finished, he continued to come around to see me.

"To make a long story short, we fell in love. Or at least, I thought we did. We got married. It lasted only a few weeks. The whole thing was a mistake. Once he found out that just because I'd inherited this house, I was not necessarily a rich woman, he took off. Never saw him again.

"I'd already discovered I was going to have a baby. But it was good riddance to him anyway. Even though I didn't know how I was going to manage on my own.

"My older sister Agnes sent me the money to go and stay with her and her husband down east, until after the baby was born. They longed to have a child. Agnes was ten years older than me, already past thirty, and had been told by that time that there would be no children for them.

"She and her husband agreed to help me, but on one condition. They would adopt the child and raise it as their own. He was never to know they were not his real parents."

Aunt Caroline looked into Norah's stricken face. "I know, Norah. My sister drove a hard bargain. But in the end, it seemed the only solution. It was the 1940s. Things were different for single women with children then. I would just come back here, and my life would carry on as it had before I met my husband, William Bolt."

"That was his name, then?" Norah asked, in a small voice.

"He said I was the only one who ever called him William." Caroline Stoppard gave one of her characteristic snorts. "Billy Bolt! Now shouldn't that have told me something?"

"What happened to Mr. Bolt?" Ginny asked. "Joseph's real father."

"I heard a couple of years after he left that he had died. Trying to jump a train, they said. Which seems a particularly foolish thing to do. But maybe he was still running away from his responsibilities. Someone found my name amongst his things and wrote to tell me that he was dead.

"Anyway, I got on with my life, tried to forget I had a son growing up in the Maritimes. Once in a while, as the years passed, I heard from Joseph—dutiful letters to 'Auntie,' thanking me for a birthday card or something. Right up until Agnes died, then nothing."

Uncle Richard spoke into the stunned silence that followed the woman's confession. "But Caroline, why would your nephew—okay, your son—choose to come to this place to spend his convalescence?" He looked as bewildered as the rest of the group.

"The climate here was warm and dry," Aunt Caroline explained. "And in those days, some people thought that made a difference in recovering from the illness. As far as Joseph knew, I was just his aunt with a convenient house in the country."

"And the strange boy?" Uncle Richard prompted. "Where does he come in?"

"Joseph told me that there was a boy who came to keep him company while he was here. I never saw him. After Joseph was well enough to go back to university, he left here, and a boy started hanging around the place. Although he never told me so, I figured he was connected in some way to Joseph, that my son didn't want me to be alone.

"I remember Joseph asking me one time, 'Will you be lonely, Auntie, when I leave?' And what did I reply? That there'd be little time for loneliness; that I would be returning to my work."

Her bitter tone turned to one of sorrow. "Oh, if Joseph ever knew I was his mother, I hope he forgave me."

"Forgave you? There was nothing to forgive," Ginny told her, with assurance. "Agnes and her husband gave your son a good, stable home. You wouldn't have been able to do that. And Joe always spoke so fondly of Agnes and Clifford. I know he loved them."

"Mother!" Norah demanded. "How much of this did you already know?"

Ginny's smile was wistful. "Your father told me years ago that his real mother was Caroline Stoppard, the woman he grew up thinking was his aunt."

To Caroline she said, "Agnes had told him the truth, dear, on her deathbed. He said he wrote and told you that your sister had died. He waited to hear if you had anything you wanted to tell him. When he heard nothing further from you, he knew you wanted to keep your secret. Rather than embarrass you, he left it alone.

"It was only after I found out we were moving here to Ontario that I decided to see if his 'Aunt' Caroline was still living in Pinegrove. I thought our visit this Christmas might be a good opportunity to ease into our family connections. If it didn't happen," Ginny said with a shrug, "so be it."

"It was finding the play and putting it on for you tonight that brought everything out in the open," Norah realized. "Could the play really have been in this house all the time, ever since my father was staying here? What a coincidence that we found it now!"

Aunt Caroline looked doubtful. "Too much of a coincidence," she said. "I may not be much of a housekeeper, but in four decades I'm sure I'd have come across it, if it were here. Besides, Joseph didn't use those upstairs rooms where you found his play. He slept down here, used the washroom near the front door. No, there has to be another explanation for how it got into this house."

Twenty-one

I haven't seen the boy in at least ten years." Aunt Caroline continued her story as if she was thinking out loud. "I thought he had given up on me and left for good. But ever since Norah…"

"Given up on you?" Andrew interrupted. He was sitting next to Norah, cross-legged on the floor in front of the old lady's loveseat. "What did he want from you?"

"He wanted me to admit the truth, I think."

"Well, I'm thoroughly confused," announced Auntie Gwen, pushing Becca off her lap and onto her feet.

Aunt Caroline turned to her and spoke slowly, choosing her words with care. She had regained her usual composure. "As I said, after Joseph returned home to finish university, I started seeing a strange boy around here. The first time he appeared on the property, I tried to shoo him away, told him he was trespassing.

"He did leave that day, but a little later on when I looked up, I saw him through the window. He had come into the garden again, and I watched him set something on the steps of the gazebo. He was waiting at the edge of the trees when I went out to see what it was. He smiled at me and nodded, letting me know that it was for me. It was a beautiful birdfeeder.

"I realized then that he meant me no harm, and after that he became my silent companion. I never knew when to expect him, but from time to time when I went outside to work in my garden, he'd be there. And he was always the same—always just a boy. I got older, but he never did."

"Impossible!" Uncle Richard blustered.

Caroline Stoppard went on with the story, ignoring the interruption. "The reason I was so sure he was connected to Joseph's stay here was because of the boy Joseph said came to visit him. He tried to point him out to me at the time, but I thought the poor man was hallucinating. I certainly didn't see whatever it was he was seeing. Not then."

"And now he's here again," said Andrew. "But Norah's the one who's seeing him."

"You are?" Ginny gasped. "Really, Norah?"

"I've seen a boy here several times," said Norah. "Talked to him, even. I thought it was weird that he knew so much about you, Aunt Caroline. But he said his family was from around here."

"Which is true," Andrew pointed out. "This was his grandparents' house." He became thoughtful. "So okay, at the end of the play, the boy gives the young man a birdfeeder. Did that really happen?"

"It did," Aunt Caroline affirmed. "Just when Joseph was ready to leave, *someone* gave him a birdfeeder. I didn't know at the time where it came from. But Joseph said it was a gift from the boy, asked me if I'd hang it out in the garden. I wanted him to take it, but he insisted on leaving it here.

"After the boy left me my first one at the gazebo, a new birdfeeder would appear in the yard every once in a while. Again and again, I asked in town about the boy, but no one knew anything about him. No one else saw him coming and going, and the people looked at me as if I was crazy. Then one day, I realized he wasn't coming any longer.

"When the boy stopped coming, so did the birdfeeders. I've bought new ones to replace those that deteriorated over the years. But none of them was as unique as the first ones—all handmade, with the most intricate detail."

"I think Jody makes them himself," said Norah. "He gets the material from the lumberyard in the village. And now I'm positive it was Jody who left the new one on the back step. For me."

"Jody?" Ginny queried. "Then he's still here?"

"He must be. And that's his name. He told me himself."

"I thought his name was Jamie." Auntie Gwen was still puzzled.

"Only in the play," Norah told her. "The young man in the play is James. His younger self is nicknamed Jamie. In real life, Jody must be a nickname for Joseph."

"It is," Ginny confirmed. "Joe told me Agnes used to call him Jody when he was a child. He didn't like the name much."

"Maybe he inherited my aversion to nicknames," observed Aunt Caroline.

"But what about the special hospital in the play," Becca asked, "and the nurse? Where were they?"

"I think the nurse in the play was supposed to be me," explained Aunt Caroline. "I took time off work to look after Joseph. But there was no hospital. It all took place right here." She looked off into the distance, a small smile playing at the corners of her mouth. "I can still see him sitting out there in the sunshine, with his pencils and paper. I had a folding lounge, and I'd take it out onto the patio for him. He'd work out there for hours. I didn't know he was sketching; I thought he was writing. I expect that was when he wrote this play."

"Maybe he wasn't sketching," Andrew suggested. "Maybe he changed that for the play, the same way he changed the names of the characters and made the setting a convalescent hospital."

"Maybe," Norah realized, picking up Andrew's train of thought, her voice rising as it dawned on her, "it wasn't a drawing that he gave the boy before he left at all, but a little play he'd been writing while he was here!"

"I bet you're right!" exclaimed Andrew.

"Wait a minute!" cried Becca, slapping her hands to her cheeks. "If the boy had only been imaginary, he wouldn't have been able to leave something real behind, like the birdfeeder. Would he? So he had to be real!"

"He is real," vowed Norah.

For a few moments everyone sat very still, trying to absorb Caroline Stoppard's amazing story, aware of the clatter of dishes coming from the kitchen, where Uncle Richard had gone to prepare refreshments. For once,

Aunt Caroline didn't seem to object.

"I have something I think you should have, Virginia," she said, addressing Norah's mother. "It's a photograph of Joseph that Agnes sent me years ago when he was three. He's sitting on a pony, pleased as punch, wearing his little cowboy outfit. I want you to have it now. I am sure I can find a frame to fit it, amongst my things."

"That's very sweet of you," murmured Ginny, her eyes bright. "I knew Joe had had TB, years before we met," she went on. "He'd been in a sanitarium until the disease was no longer infectious, and I remember he said he had to be on medication for about eighteen months afterwards. But I never knew he ever stayed here."

"Oh, yes. All one autumn," said Aunt Caroline. "Lying out there in the sun, building up his strength. And to think I never told him the truth about his parentage! Oh, I was tempted, but I never did. I had promised Agnes that I wouldn't." She sighed. "And then he was gone.

"As you said, Virginia, he let me know some years later that Agnes had died, and that's the last time we communicated. I never knew until you wrote, my dear, introducing yourself as Joseph Bingham's widow and inviting me to share Christmas with you, whether he had married or if he had a family."

"Joe was past forty when we got married," Ginny told her. "He died when Norah was almost three, ten years ago now."

Aunt Caroline's white head was nodding. "Yes, that would be just about the time I stopped seeing him—the boy, I mean. That would explain why he didn't come any more."

"So there really was a boy named Jamie?" Auntie Gwen took a cup of eggnog from the tray Uncle Richard was offering.

"Jody, apparently," Uncle Richard scoffed. "And he's got to be over sixty! There's no way he's still a boy. Unless he's Peter Pan!"

Great-aunt Caroline shot Uncle Richard a withering look. "Whether or not the boy is real is a moot point," she said. "It doesn't matter."

"But who was he really?" Becca asked.

"He was my father," said Norah. "Or at least, the boy who would grow up to be my father. I wish I'd known that when I met him. Think of all the things I could've asked him!"

"I think you, Norah, are the reason he is here now," said Aunt Caroline. "To remind me I have another chance, one more opportunity to acknowledge who he was and to reconnect with the family I have left. And without Joseph's little play, I might have missed it."

Twenty-two

The three children spent the evening feasting on the popcorn and cocoa that Caroline Stoppard set out for them on the table in the dining room. The adults, with the exception of the old lady, had gone to church in the village.

But Norah was restless. Again and again she went to the window to look out at the dark forest beyond the yard. Several times she lifted the birdfeeder from the buffet and read Jody's inscription on the bottom.

"I bet that'll be your favourite present this year," Andrew predicted, wiping butter off his chin.

Caroline Stoppard gathered the empty mugs from the table. "Isn't it about time you three were in bed?" she asked.

"Mom said I could stay up till they get back," said Becca. "Besides, I can never get to sleep on Christmas Eve."

"I shall have no trouble sleeping tonight, whatsoever," Caroline Stoppard declared. She glared at Norah. "What is the matter, Norah? You've been pacing around here for the past hour."

Norah turned from the window and looked steadily into her grandmother's eyes. "I won't see the boy again, will I? I won't ever be able to say thank you."

"I think he knows," Caroline Stoppard said, in a gentler tone. "His mission has been accomplished."

"I just feel bad about not having a present for him," Norah admitted.

"I'm sure he doesn't expect one," said Andrew.

"That doesn't matter. He left me something."

"But you didn't know he would," Becca pointed out.

"Well, let me see," said Caroline Stoppard, taking them all by surprise. Her eyes swept the room. "Is there anything I might have around here that you'd like to give him?"

"Oh, really? Could I?"

"Surely. Look here." Norah's grandmother picked up the snow globe from the buffet where it had been sitting ever since Andrew and Becca had given it to her. "What about this?"

Norah shot a quick glance at her cousins. "But it's yours," she reminded the woman.

"Now, really! What's an old lady going to do with something like that?"

"Is that why you don't have any pictures or pretty things in your house?" Becca asked. "Because you are an old lady?"

"Becca!" Colour flared in Andrew's cheeks, and Norah held her breath.

"No, Rebecca," Caroline Stoppard replied evenly. "I took the pictures down because my heart was sad. I didn't think I deserved to look at such pretty things.

"This present you and your brother gave me was a lovely thought. And that was its purpose. But now it can be another lovely thought. You don't mind, do you, Rebecca? Andrew?"

"I think it's perfect," said Andrew.

Becca jumped up from the table. "Me too!" she cried. "Where will we leave it so he'll be sure to find it?"

"Right on the back step," Norah decided. "Where Jody left the birdfeeder."

"Ooh, can I take it out?" Becca was already halfway through the door to the kitchen.

"We'll all go," said Norah. "Ready, Grandmother?"

"Wouldn't miss this for the world," declared Caroline Stoppard.

*   *   *

Norah rolled over next morning and discovered Ginny had already gone downstairs. The homey smell of coffee and toast wafted into the bedroom. What time was it, anyway? Never in her whole life had she slept in on Christmas morning.

She sat up abruptly. The snow globe! Would Jody have found it?

Seconds later, shoving her arms through the sleeves of her bathrobe, Norah hurried down the stairs. Her mother and Auntie Gwen were setting the table in the dining room. Uncle Richard poured coffee into a mug and handed it to Caroline Stoppard. The old lady was already seated at the table and looking a little indignant at being waited on.

"Merry Christmas, everybody," Norah called, scurrying

through the room.

"Hey, sleepyhead," Uncle Richard greeted her. "We wondered when you'd be up."

"Where are you going?"

"Outside a minute. I'll be right back." Norah pushed through the door to the kitchen.

"But you're not even dressed!" Ginny pointed out.

"It's just snow, after all."

"You'll ruin your slippers," Auntie Gwen warned.

"Leave her be," snapped Caroline Stoppard. "The children and I know what it is she's looking for."

Norah opened the back door and stepped outside.

Her present to Jody was gone. Only a circle remained in the snow on the back step, marking the place where the snow globe had been. Norah stood there for a long minute, feeling the smile grow wide across her face.

*   *   *

The morning was crisp and cold. It was time to leave; Jody's job was done.

Last night he'd stood in the snow, in the patch of coloured light behind the Stoppard house, and watched the happy gathering inside. Jody knew then that this chance to reunite his family was what had called him to come back.

Jody patted the place where Norah's present lay nestled, deep in the pocket of his jacket, and closed the door of the little shed behind him.

Photo by Chris McArthur

Born in Toronto, Peggy Dymond Leavey began writing as a child and has published poems, articles and plays for both adults and children. She has collaborated on three books of local history and has done freelance writing. Her first novel for children, *Help Wanted: Wednesdays Only*, was published in 1994 by Napoleon Publishing. *A Circle in Time* was published in 1994, also by Napoleon. Her third book, *Sky Lake Summer*, published in 1999, was nominated for a Silver Birch Award and a Manitoba Young Readers' Choice Award.

Peggy's first teen novel, *Finding My Own Way*, was published by Napoleon in the fall of 2001. It was followed by another junior novel, *The Deep End Gang*, in 2003, which was an honour finalist for the Silver Birch Award. *The Path Through the Trees* is her sixth novel for young readers. Today, Peggy lives near Trenton, Ontario, with her husband.